Are You Ready to Be Lucky?

Books by Rosemary Nixon

Mostly Country
The Cock's Egg
Kalila

Are You Ready to Be Lucky?

ROSEMARY NIXON

Canada Council **Conseil des Arts**
for the Arts **du Canada**

Freehand Books gratefully acknowledges the support of the Canada
Council for the Arts for its publishing program. ¶ Freehand Books, an
imprint of Broadview Press Inc., acknowledges the financial support for
its publishing program provided by the Government of Canada through
the Canada Book Fund.

Freehand Books
515–815 1st Street SW Calgary, Alberta T2P 1N3
www.freehand-books.com

Book orders: LitDistCo
100 Armstrong Avenue Georgetown, Ontario L7G 5S4
Telephone: 1-800-591-6250 Fax: 1-800-591-6251
orders@litdistco.ca
www.litdistco.ca

Library and Archives Canada Cataloguing In Publication
Nixon, Rosemary
    Are you ready to be lucky? / Rosemary Nixon.
Short stories.
Also issued in electronic format.
ISBN 978-1-55481-138-0
    1. Title.
PS8577.I95A74 2013   C813'.54   C2013-901665-1

Edited by Barbara Scott
Book design by Natalie Olsen, kisscutdesign.com
Author photo by Tory James

Printed on FSC recycled paper and bound in Canada

This is a work of fiction and any resemblance to persons living or dead is coincidental.

For Lloyd C. Filimek

master builder, friend

Are You Ready to Be Lucky?

========

Roslyn high-steps up Bantry Street on an icy Alberta evening buffeted by late-December gusts, holding high her sixty by forty centimetre tray of pineapple-stuffed meatballs, trying not to look like a woman who, at the yearly No Commitment Book Club Christmas gift exchange, received a can of gravy and two books called *How to Seem Like a Better Person Without Actually Improving Yourself* and *The Zombie Survival Guide: Complete Protection from the Living Dead.* Roslyn steps lively, though it's difficult through this latest dump of snow. By the time she's crossing 10th Street at the four-way stop, she's trying out the mien of a woman whose sashay declares, Hey! I've spent time in Peru! A guy in a woollen toque with strings, behind the wheel of a Honda Accord, honks. Is it working, then, or is he just pissed off she isn't trotting? Roslyn plods faster. She fears there's an air about her, a colloquial cast that reveals she's never set foot off the North American continent. By the time she turns down Russet Road, she's practicing nice-but-not-sexually-conservative. She imagines popping out of a giant toaster, singing gustily, "Butter Me Baby!" Sexy, but spritzed with positive attitude, so the faces of those watching her streak from lustful to inspired — *Look at you!* — dolloped with fascination at her role-modelling magnetism. She passes the burnt-orange house with the seven small windmills, where Stella, toward whose party Roslyn is trudging, says the mom sells pot. Well, Stella would know. Roslyn tries to look like the kind of person who is fun, yet speaks encouragingly to people. Six weeks since her divorce. Does she look divorced? Well, look it or not, she and Harold are kaput. Life lurches on. She skids off a sidewalk so snow-covered she wasn't expecting its edge. Roslyn pictures herself a potted plant, flinging its diseased parts forth for pruning. Parts that twined Harold for twenty-three years. Harold who, for their last vacation together, booked a hotel in Seattle with a dog-eared *Playboy* under the bed and lice within it. And then he left her. Before his exit, the two of them, colliding under Roslyn's ricocheting umbrella, walked Wanda who, terrified by Seattle's concrete, refused to pee, ululating in bladder discomfort. Harold, pushing his voice above the yipping and the wind, shared with Roslyn (and a passing woman with a package of fish and a receding hairline) that he'd slept with a woman at a boner convention six months before, and how much he'd liked her feet. Harold is manager of a company that inserts stays called bones into prepared pockets of women's foundation garments. "I told her," Harold explained, as Wanda emitted a series of anguished squirts, "if you could see inside my head, you'd realize how un-attracted I've become to my wife." Harold values honesty. What a quality! "Did you say *unattractive* to your wife?" Roslyn asked, but the damp Seattle sea breeze hurled her words, cloaked in pee-spray, against a derelict public transit building.

For twenty-three years Roslyn tolerated Harold's insistence on perfect grammar. His mother was a high school English teacher. Mix "me" and "I" in a prepositional phrase and Harold sulked for days. She tolerated his penchant for inquiring mornings if she'd used his toothbrush. Just checking! His grandpa's family on his mother's side had had a hired man who used the family's toothbrushes for weeks before a telltale splotch of Kits Taffy on Harold's grandma's nailed the rotter. For twenty-three years Roslyn watched Harold stride grimly from the room each time she bit into an apple or a carrot. Tolerated his growing addiction for the purchase of eBay items they'd never use: a canoe, a hundred taped-together boxes of saran wrap, rat poison. Rat poison, when they live in the only rat-free province in the country. Well, here Roslyn is, a forty-two-year-old divorcée on her way to Stella's *Eyes Wide Shut* New Year's Eve party. Damn it! A woman can only bawl so long. With luck Stella's kept on her meds.

Roslyn blows across Remington Road and climbs Stella's pink-encrusted front steps. Stella had a short-lived summer fling with a feng shui instructor who took off after nine days, wishing her blessings. Said he was headed to Hidden Valley Ashram to contemplate entering a monastery. He left behind a pile of rose quartz stones that Stella had a workman embed in new concrete steps — her wooden ones were rotting. "Rose quartz brings luck," Stella told Roslyn. "Rose quartz is a love stone." Roslyn had been standing in Stella's kitchen, gulping her homemade lemonade without sugar. Stella was doing a *Look Better Naked Organic Herbal Colon Cleanse*. She was face down, hovering just above the floorboards, trying to hold plank position for a minute and a half. "Rose quartz *attracts* love, Roz," Stella had gasped. And sure enough, didn't Stella have a fling with the man who redid the stairs.

Whoops! Roslyn slips on the stones' slick surface. Her tray of pineapple-stuffed meatballs skids, teeters, and a meatball plops at her feet like an enthusiastic turd. Roslyn pivots — no one watching — scoops it up and sticks it back against its smudge on the tray. The streetlight gives a white-light-otherworldly glow to the pink translucent chips. Despite herself, a funnel of excitement plows through Roslyn's goose-pimpled skin toward her coffee-dregged heart. A series of chances. That's what life is. A Russian roulette of heartbreak and passion. Click. Hear that? The spin of the revolver's cylinder. Maybe her time has come. Roslyn scrapes boot soles against the pink quartz to dislodge hardened snow clumps. Has she not risen from the crumb-laden crying-nest of her unmade bed? In four hours it will be a New Year. Roslyn bends over her meatballs, holds her finger to the bell. Stella's invitation said, Costume Party. Roslyn pulls a cigarillo from her pocket. She's come as a knock-out cowgirl.

The door swings open to a wallop of moist heat, wafting curry, and a technicolour Stella, buck-naked, body-painted in hues of tangerine, turquoise, and green. "Welcome!" Stella twirls her hand and bends in a sweeping bow. "Jeez, Roz.

Shut the goddamn door!" Roslyn hands over her tray of spongy globes, each impaled with its own toothpick.

Stella squints at the tray. "Meatballs. Not feeling great, I take it."

"Like a bunion," Roslyn says cheerfully. "But an early-stage one — whose time has come." She relinquishes her coat, keeps on her cowboy boots, clips into Stella's tackily-decorated living room, and stands very still on the makeshift party dancefloor. She squeezes her eyes tight shut and — Whooooot! — blows Harold, the boner, like a smoke ring, from her life. Then she turns with — hopefully — an air of carefree abandon, only to be run amok by a gentleman gyrating gustily across the dancefloor in the arms of Shirley Turlington, nursemaid costume riding her chubby thighs. Shirley Turlington, who brought a ten-dollar bottle opener as her gift to the No Commitment Book Club Christmas gift exchange, and took home an eighty-five-dollar boxed set of steak knives. But what's this? A distinctly British voice saying, "Blimey! Were you waiting for the aeroplane? Let's get you off the runway!" And yes, Shirley Turlington, nurse's hat askew, is left to bebop ungracefully off the dancefloor, *seule,* while Duncan Bloxham, Yorkshireman — for so he introduces himself — reaches a manicured hand to help Roslyn up, apologizing, laughing heartily, touching her hands, holding them really, exclaiming that they are bloody cold, and where did she get such a get-up, she needs a man like him to dress her. He winks. The man actually winks. Oh his voice! That accent! But Roslyn has barely staggered to her feet before Stella is dragging her into the kitchen, and propping her against the devilled egg tray on the counter, Stella's nipples rising indignantly like the avocado wedge tips standing guard atop the devilled eggs. "I only invited him because Tamai met him on the ski slope." Stella clutches Roslyn's arm, leaving tangerine residue. "We don't know anything about him!"

A gentle bump against the kitchen's swinging door. A shadow looms beneath it.

"The man took over my chocolate mousse!" Stella whispers. "Told me I was shaving the chocolate curls incorrectly! What kind of man thinks chocolate curls can be shaved *correctly?!*" Roslyn wrenches free, takes three quick tiptoes, and swings open the swinging door. Duncan Bloxham, mid-sprint across the living room floor, halts in a stance of frozen tag. He recovers, strikes a pondering pose, nose lifted, and flicks his coral sweater over his rounded shoulder.

"Eavesdropper!" Roslyn calls. Duncan grins, and tips his glass in her direction. The last wisps of Harold, the boner, bob bob bob away.

§

Shirley Turlington, read 'er and weep. Duncan Bloxham chooses Roslyn from all the women at Stella's party because: 1. she keeps her clothes on; 2. she has warm tints in her hair that remind Duncan of his dead mother's; 3. at 2:14 a.m. she climbs on a dining room chair and, alongside a platter of Wilhemina Wyvil's soda-cracker-lemon squares tossed with people's abandoned pizza crusts, she belts, a capella, "Walk Right Back"; and 4. because Bill Gerard raves drunkenly that she shone up there like a Roman candle.

The Yorkshireman agrees. Under the mistletoe, Duncan Bloxham kisses Roslyn's eyelids. One. Two. They slow dance to "Count on Me."

§

"So Canadians live in extended dog kennels then?" Duncan says, good-naturedly mystified, eight days after Stella's party, the day he moves in. He stands in Roslyn's living room, inspecting the splatterings of water-drool between the dog dish and Wanda, who barks once, skulks around the filing cabinet, and dives under Roslyn's study desk where she stays while the rest of Duncan's suitcases thump on Roslyn's porch, darting out just once to defiantly guzzle a second sloppy drink. Extended dog kennel! What a funny guy! This man's dry wit is hilarious, his accent sexy as hell, his dress sense splendo-chic! Roslyn records his line in her journal along with other tidbits of Duncan Bloxham's adorable speech — *I can't be bothered, That's not on! Your streets go higgledy-piggledy! I'm just sat-sitting* — while Duncan trots smartly by in a Gucci light blue poplin dress shirt and grey wool trousers, with pleats, balancing a sudsy bucket, heading for Roslyn's driveway and the car she put through the carwash just three days before.

"It's winter, Duncan! The doors will freeze!"

"It's streaky! A car wants to shine!"

He scrubbed, rinsed, and turtle-waxed his car, then Harriet's, back in England, every Sunday afternoon at two, finishing at four forty-five, just in time for tea. What a catch! Roslyn phones her sister with the news.

Nights they curl up on the couch sharing gin and tonics — Roslyn's not much of a drinker, but she practices her Lauren Bacall impersonation, loftily sipping — while Duncan makes delightful fun of the American newscasters with their identical comb-over blond coifs. Roslyn climbs her pedestal. Seats herself on its embroidered pillow. What comfort! What a view! Duncan buys her yellow freesia and crimson gerbera flowers. Roslyn lets him beat her at Scrabble. He rubs her feet. Duncan, it turns out, despite his good-natured mockery, is *fond* of flannel pyjamas. He buys Wanda elk liver nuggets despite her ensuing dreadful farts. He buys Roslyn designer clothes. He rubs *Wanda*'s feet. Roslyn adores this man. How did she get so lucky? And Theo? Well, actually, Roslyn hasn't mentioned Duncan yet to Theo. She will. Of course she will. He's twenty-two, coming twenty-three, just the age where you'd rather not think of your mother in love. Still stinging a bit from the divorce. This may be too soon — besides, he's on a ski holiday with his buddies. She'll get to it. Each day Duncan finds new reasons to admire Roslyn and Wanda. Let him count the ways! Roslyn's ability to cry sharp, authoritative commands, Wanda's to shake a paw, to flip on her back, poking four stiff paws in the air at the cry of "Wanda! Would you rather be Duncan — or DEAD?!"

The holiday ends. Duncan, Roslyn discovers — there is so much to discover about Duncan — took early retirement in England, despite Harriet's protestations. So Harriet had an affair; the marriage ended. Duncan spends his days devotedly reading the *Globe and Mail* to learn about his new country, watching reruns, downloading songs, shovelling the sidewalk. Settling in to Canadian ways. Some nights he shouts out in his sleep, angry unintelligible pronouncements. It's part of leaving so much behind.

"You don't need to work." He rubs her shoulders. Insists she take a break from teaching foreign students. At least take the term off. They can spend time together. So much shopping to do. However, when Duncan learns that for the last few years she's taken a second job each Christmas season — money for extras — when he learns which job that is, Duncan's enthusiasm rockets. Well, yes! By all means! Keep working part time. Just to hold her foot in the door.

When Roslyn gets home from La Senza those first nights to a sparkling house, and reordered cupboards, there's Duncan, perched expectantly on the edge of her loveseat (a name that sends him into choking insufflations), in his boxers, eyes anticipatorily green. Roslyn hangs her coat in the dark hall closet, snuggles in beside him, and launches into her day's duties for Duncan's listening pleasure. Fanning. Colour blocking. Hands deep all day in women's sexy underwear. Duncan's fingers already plunged in hers. Fanning and colour blocking take no small skill — Duncan yanks Roslyn's Very Berry Embroidered Deep Plunge Bra over her head, heedless of the clasp. Her breasts spring forth friskily. The seams on the Sunkist Mist must be perfectly aligned with the seams of the Vervi Violet aligned with the seams of the Blush Me Scarlet — Snap! goes Roslyn's No Show Jewel Mauve thong. A whoosh of cool air. Keep going, Roslyn! Tell him more! The Petites fan the table front, the Mediums the middle. Ohhh. Larges lounge at the back. She has perfected fanning. So has Duncan Bloxham. His fingers skittering, bobbing, frisking, tickling, hippety hop! The floor of La Senza, croaks Roslyn to the back of Duncan's head — his face now disappeared below her belly button — is a cross between a boudoir, and — oooh — jail. All those scattered bits of underwear — Duncan's anguished yelping. Oh! Oh! Ohhhhh! Duncan, boisterously accordioning her breasts, emitting high-pitched barks, Wanda's shoving wet nose making a threesome — all those clerks with all those dressing room keys — Criiiii-keeeeey! A flushed, boyish, damp-faced Duncan, swatting at nipping Wanda, tumbles off the sofa, his asthmatic wheezes fanning the flames of the grapefruit candles he's set out on the coffee table for atmosphere.

"Bloody brilliant!" he moans, head wedged between the coffee table and the couch foot, the flames of the candles, like Roslyn, blinking: on-off-on. "Aren't you something!"

Yowza. Lady Luck has moseyed in.

Repeat tomorrow.

Week three: Roslyn walks in the door at the end of her evening shift to find a blotchy-faced Duncan started in on an assembly line of scotches. Harriet has called. Scotch number three. Where does Roslyn really go between six and ten? Scotch number four. Duncan'll get to the bottom of this. Oh yeah! Watch yourself, Missy! He eyeballs her mournfully through an alcoholic miasma. Why *is* Roslyn twenty-three minutes late? Why *did* no one answer the phone when Duncan repeatedly called the shop an hour ago? Why *does* she smell like Jean-Paul Gaultier cologne?

Bloody hell. He's sorry, Duncan moans, moments after a predawn romp, his fingers teasing their way around Roslyn's pyjama elastic. It was hearing Harriet's voice. Out of nowhere swooped the stress, the grief, the fighting, all he's lost. But oh, how Roslyn helps him leave it all behind — No. No! He doesn't mistrust her. NOT. AT. ALL! He licks her enthusiastically. He loves her! She reminds him of his mother. No! Not like *that!* His mother in her youth. Black-and-white forties movie star kind of woman. His mother was *glamorous*. He kisses Roslyn's neck, her ear, her elbow.

Week five: Tonight when Roslyn steps in the door after another quick coffee with Theo — she'll tell him any day now, she just hasn't found the moment — she can barely make out Duncan's doleful form listing on the loveseat. Duncan's big on extinguishing the lights. Economy, not romance. If Roslyn walks from the sofa into her study nights to grab a book, she'll be feeling her way back a moment later into a room plunged into darkness. Her house, along with her dog, has taken on a furtive air.

"Hi!" she says to this man sunk into her cushions. *Why is he here?* She has to remind herself lately how chance led him to her living room sofa. Harriet dreamed of the pristine Rockies the way British children dream of hoarhound candy. So, buoyed by adventure (and a smidgeon of revenge), Duncan took himself off to a travel agent, crossed the pond, and discovered Banff, which he pronounces Ban-aff — and

Roslyn. There's the scotch. There are Duncan's feet up on Roslyn's coffee table because feet-on-the-coffee-table is what Canadians do.

Duncan pats the seat beside him. "Everybody grins all the time," he complains, waving at the beaming news announcer on the flickering television. "A person can only take so much grinning!" Roslyn pokers her face and sits. The weatherman genuflects past his map, gleefully forecasting snow. Duncan sighs. He's beginning to take snow personally. Scrabbling through it like a dog. Morosely hurling shovelfuls of the gravel-speckled salt-and-pepper clumps over his shoulder, as if hopelessly flinging away bad luck before the next dump, while Roslyn jogs blithely into winter's faded light, frost cracking like gunshots beneath her treads, a habit that Duncan finds absurd, this racing off for the sole purpose of ending up exactly where she started. Apparently no one in the UK has heard of the BMI. Roslyn politely ignores Duncan's nudging beer belly that can no longer be hidden beneath his suave Italian shirts. Granted, he drank too much through the divorce, but he's going to cut down, of course he'll cut down, once he gets the hang of Canada. Besides, Brits drink. That's what they do. Give Duncan time. The blow up? Well, just for those moments, he had it in his head that she was Harriet. Just a bit too much whisky combined with lack of sleep and Harriet's nasty phone call. He doesn't know how she tracked him down. Of course he didn't call first!

There he sits, like a large package the post office mistakenly delivered to her door. And if Roslyn thinks he's returning to Hull, to live in a little bedsit with stale-smelling towels and a broad-bosomed landlady on a side street well below the antediluvian stone house with its hundred-year-old brick that Harriet and "that cowboy Dwayne" snatched in the divorce, Roslyn can think again! Duncan emits a little burst of air. At Dwayne. At Harriet. At Canada's bewildering forests, its incomprehensible radio commercials, its barmy ice hockey rules, its football called soccer, its pavements called sidewalks, its penchant for potlucks, its refusal to serve chips with lasagne.

Roslyn wanders down the hall and lugs back the iron and ironing board. Duncan smiles at her bleakly and sips his whisky. The news fades to commercial during which Duncan musters enough cheer to mock Certs, while Wanda squashes herself against Roslyn's study wall in an uneasy gulping sleep, giving occasional small shrieks as if pinched.

Duncan drums his fingers on the loveseat arm, head bobbing, switches channels, and watches detectives interrogate a size zero woman with a lot of cleavage and a lip ring.

"Know how to drink single malt whisky?"

"What?!"

"Single malt whisky!"

"Put it in your mouth? Swallow?"

Aha! What a silly goose she is. Duncan will demonstrate. He jumps to his feet.

"Firstly, your glasses are all wrong. I had to buy new ones today." Duncan holds his up and taps it. "A tapered top. You want a tapered top for single malt whisky. So — pour, then hold the glass by the — you're not watching!"

Roslyn plunks down the iron on its butt.

"Hold the glass in the cup of your hand. See? This warms it, releasing the scent. Now this part: this is called 'The

Nosing.'" Duncan lifts his own, sticks it over the glass, and takes a deep whiff. Wanda sits up in alarm.

"The body — are you with me? — your whisky wants to be amber, the colour of honey. *Meadow* honey."

Minutes later, Duncan's heading toward what he calls "The Finish Line." "This is called 'Swishing,'" and he swings into what appears to be a vigorous ad for Listerine.

"Now a lesser man adds water —"

"Duncan. I don't care!"

"You have an I-don't-care attitude!" Duncan slams the glass down. Wanda yelps. Roslyn's clock chimes ten. "I'm trying to teach you class, but here you are, pratting about ironing. Doesn't matter! What does it matter I'd appreciate a drink together after a long day alone. You got out. That's what's important. No! No! Just have your water."

Wanda dog-tracks to the back door and stands, head bowed as if ashamed she has to poo. When Roslyn opens the door, Wanda leaps out as if electric-shocked, squeezes through a hole in the neighbour's fence, and bites the snow-man.

"What shall we do tomorrow?"

"I'm getting my hair cut."

"Of course. Of course. Why wouldn't you."

"And then Stella and I are going for lunch —"

"Oh! You're running off for lunch now? Anything else I don't know about? Well, there's Friday gone. Corking!"

The stricken look staining his face makes rise in Roslyn a kind of ancient maternal longing, followed by a tingling through her entire body. So far from home. Of course she wants him to stay. Needs him to stay. Of course she forgives him. It takes time, getting used to the jolt of life without one's family, getting used to a strange country, each other. Roslyn runs the iron over Duncan's cotton boxers. Besides, this is love. By the time Duncan has changed into his kimono-style silk pyjamas covered in foxes, his fingers will be deliciously coasting her inner thighs. She will abandon the spitting iron, and Duncan Bloxham, teetering on his belly, will tongue her to ecstasy. Sex, which, according to Duncan, Harriet gave in to on bank holidays and Guy Fawkes Day, keeps Duncan Bloxham adjusting, fixing, cleansing, mending, renovating, thrilling her. Besides, it's exhilarating how she can make him forget for moments, sometimes days, Harriet's deluge of calls — collect — during which she shouts that their son James's roommate is threatening to move out because James, traumatized by Duncan's departure, keeps ranting into the fry pan and refusing to cook any vegetable but Brussels sprouts, can make him forget Harriet's angry breathing while Duncan fast-talks before she slams the receiver down, forget that all his tools are still hanging in his garage at "that cowboy Dwayne's" disposal, tools needing 220 volts, so it's pointless stealing them back.

If Roslyn answers the telephone, Harriet says, "Who's this?" as if Duncan rotates Canadian women through the house like winter tires. Roslyn hands over the receiver and a good fifty minutes later Duncan gets off the phone and has a go at her for owning so many books, for having café latte walls instead of lilac wallpaper. For smelling like butter tarts. Sometimes he veers into a go at her for running Harriet down.

"But she was having an affair, Duncan! A ten-month affair!"

"What would you know? You've never even met her!"

"You mean you made it up?"

"You weren't even there!"

He ends by having a go at Canada's scarcity of road signs, the lack of drunks in the street. He finds this absence ridiculous. What do you people do for fun?

True — at times her love squeezes into a small steel wrecking ball that slams beneath her ribcage. But mostly Roslyn's not that bothered. It's kind of endearing, Duncan's absurdity, followed, like clockwork, by guilt, remorse, such need to make it up to her. How he goes on! How lovely she is. How good to him. How wonderful Canadians are. What *would* he do without her? He'd be lost. *Lost!* This country has brought him to life. Here — he's bought her a little something: a silver ring, a cashmere scarf, a Christian Louboutin clutch — he found an online sale . . .

It's nothing but a stage. This melancholy Lord Byron tethered to her sofa. Grievers go through stages, don't they? — denial, bargaining, depression, anger, brief bouts of insanity — doesn't he always fight his way back to his delightful witty self? See? There he is already, sweet-faced, beckoning her from the hall, pyjamas on, that little hopeful grin warming the lines and creases. Of course it's not easy. Who knows better than Roslyn? He'll pull through. Sure, it's possible that Duncan's defection to Canada *originally* might have had something to do with butting Harriet into taking him back. Sure the thought's occurred to Roslyn. But it's becoming clear, even to Duncan, that "that cowboy Dwayne" has got his clutches deep in Harriet *and* the house.

Duncan won't be getting back into either.

Give the man time. He'll let go of his obsession. He'll come around.

Week nine: Sunday morning. The phone rings, six a.m. Harriet's forte isn't time zones. Duncan leaps from bed, Roslyn stumbling after in her Fast-a-Sheep Glow-in-the-Dark baby dolls. She gets a hefty La Senza discount. She has been waking in the night lately to Duncan clawing her legs, his arms snaking her back, trying to get himself inside her in his sleep.

"Oh, right! You and Dwayne are flying to Spain for Easter holiday? Ryanair? A seat sale? That is *not* a good price. Well, it isn't is it? I can so. I will so. Yeah? Well guess what? I'm *moving* to Spain. We're *buying* there. I am not. Yes we are! Where do you think? On the Costa Blanca! Right where you've always dreamed of your holiday house, Harriet! That's where *we're* going!"

Holy Canoly! Roslyn grabs the kitchen counter, mouth-breathing in the dark. She's going to be a European traveller! She'll have to leave her job! No more clients tracking snow and mud, flinging undergarments that she must spend hours re-fanning, only to find they've flung them all again; no more boyfriends finger-smudging the glass shelves by the checkout counter, lifting and dropping the on-sale bra straps, the lingerie detergent, the fake bolster-breasts, the stay-up stockings, the candles, lip gloss, all themed to match the Bra-Set-of-the-Week. No more Stock Days: humungous boxes arriving from China with every single piece of underwear in its own individual crinkly cellophane package, Roslyn toiling under a tower of see-through recycling, the boss tottering circles in her neon-pink high heels patterned with yellow bees, insisting every bra be hung on its own hanger, all facing the same direction, perfect rows of question marks. Isn't it true that Roslyn won't be allowed to work in Europe? She'll be living a holiday! Roslyn snaps on the kitchen light and rushes for the kettle. She'll brew Duncan a nice strong pot of Tetley tea!

And then phone Theo.

Week fourteen: Roslyn and Duncan careen along in the fishtailing taxi, which has apparently already switched to summer tires, heading for the airport. It's been a wild five weeks in which Roslyn put her house on the market, sold it, got married, bought a house in Spain—a "villa," Duncan calls it—online. He'll pay her back when the sale of his house in England comes through. Telling Theo was hard. She didn't invite him to the wedding. Well, there was hardly time. Besides, it wasn't a real wedding, just her and Duncan, with Stella and her new guy as witnesses. Theo will get over it, Duncan says. Boys don't care about these things; they're into sports and girlfriends. Roslyn's sister said, "Are you crazy? Do you even know the man's middle name?!" But hasn't Roslyn always played it safe? Look where that's got her. Married at nineteen. Baby at twenty. Divorced at forty-two. The arc of her life after Harold walked out: doddering home nights to a single pork chop, curled up alone under the electric blanket.

"Duncan?" Roslyn grabs hold of his ringed hand. "My middle name is Jane."

But Duncan is bouncing about on the stiff cracked vinyl back seat of the taxicab, excitedly promising *haute culture*, flamenco dancing, *paella*, and Spanish leather.

Spain is *the* place to be, Duncan explains to the stone-faced taxi driver. He's looking to make thirty per cent by selling the villa within two years. Add to that the rising euro. "We'll be able to afford a *mansion* in Canada!" Duncan chuckles, turning to Roslyn, "should we even *wish* to return."

Theo and his new girlfriend drove up from Kamloops to take Wanda—Roslyn didn't even know he'd moved until she tried to track him down. That was a little hard. Has a job in a restaurant, he told her. Didn't say which one, just gave her a stiff hug goodbye and escorted Wanda from the premises; the girlfriend, whose name Roslyn keeps forgetting, staring backwards as they made off down the sidewalk, as if Roslyn might attack them from behind. And then they drove away, Wanda anxiously circling on the back seat, drooling up the strip of duct tape along the window crack. As the car disappeared around the corner, Roslyn experienced an inner draft, as if some central heating system had been snapped off deep inside her. She wanted to hurtle herself after Theo's rusty Ford, ululating, Doooon't gooooooo! Duncan was cheerfully sympathetic for almost an hour, then insisted they go shopping: Femme De Carrière, La Chic Ladies Wear, Naked on 17th advertising "edgy Italian designs." That gave Duncan a chuckle. Clothes, just to tide her over until he gets her into the Spanish shops. "Then I'll show you fashion. Oh, yeah."

Roslyn packed three bathing suits, her row of just-in spring sundresses: hot tangerine, lemon, lime. Packed away her sadness. And *para ti sorpresa*, they're off to Spain.

Waiting on the runway, Roslyn looks out the airplane window, past the semi-circle of frost, Duncan bavarding at her side. Silver planes, silver snow, silver sky, silver ski jackets and, bobbing in and out of her vision, Duncan's silver hair. She'll write Theo as soon as she gets there. Maybe invite him for a visit—

"Canadians have little style to speak of," Duncan is leaning forward to tell the woman across the aisle. He has worn his black silk shirt as proof. His mustard trousers. He swings his scarf. "This is Armani. I've done a European knot." The woman picks her chained glasses off her chest, and peers through them. Roslyn looks at the woman's large feet in her orthopedic shoes.

"What you will learn in the dress and shoe shops of Europe!" Duncan beams.

"I'm going to a funeral," the woman says.

"I'll be taking *my* wife," Duncan sails on. "Get her some decent clothes. You'd be astounded at the transformation. Europe, like myself, *is* fashion forward."

For the rest of the trip Roslyn studies her Spanish phrase book. Duncan drinks and sings under his breath. His passport slips out of his hand when he nods off. Roslyn retrieves it. He's lied about his age! Duncan isn't forty-nine. He's fifty-six! What an old silly to be so vain. Roslyn snuggles up beside her slightly-snoring husband, and watches the light slip past, falling to the provinces below.

Nine hours later a dried-out, sleep-deprived Roslyn and a tipsy Duncan head out of customs at Heathrow Airport, and catch the bus to Gatwick. They'll stay the night at The Flying Scud. Duncan has arranged to spend an hour at the pub with his sister's family, down from Hull. Roslyn's about to meet the relatives!

"Hull: Great Britain's Ugliest City" says an article in *The Sunday Times* that Roslyn picked up on the move through Heathrow.

"Terrific," Duncan says on the swaying bus ride when Roslyn shows it to him. He digs wax from his ear. "Of course *you'd* know."

The sister's family has driven all those hours from Yorkshire to drop their son off for auditions with a band. He's a smashing singer. Does punk, heavy metal, and all the old sixties songs. Duncan's other sister lives in Scotland. No one speaks to her.

And there they are: Duncan's baby sister and her family, waiting in the rain when Roslyn and Duncan step off the bus. Veronica: all that sagging, eager cleavage. Husband and two teenagers clustered grape-like about her to catch a glimpse of Uncle Duncan and the Canadian. Mother and daughter in matching spaghetti-strap dresses despite the chill, the filmy material barely squeezing in the wobbly bits, printed with what look like life-sized car batteries. The nephew in a T-shirt that says Motörhead. The niece's legs planted in wet spreading fuchsia ballet slippers, the sister's toes heroically squished between the straps of her high-heeled sandals sinking in the mud, umbrella launched above her head. A triumphant "Duncan!"

Duncan, cocky, grand. The benevolent uncle from Canada. A man of leisure heading to sunny Spain. The fat, adoring sister. Her tapioca-hued children. Their faces ardent and squashed-looking. The whole admiring family smelling damp and fruity.

"I'm so pleased to meet you," Roslyn says, and all four swing to Duncan in alarm. Roslyn's mouth stretches like a dog's.

The sister, the husband, and the two teenagers push in at the table as Duncan opens his laptop. The sister's hand keeps digging in her purse, but she never comes up with anything. She balances a second-hand Jaffa Cakes United Biscuit bag on her lap. Roslyn never makes out what's in it. No one bothers with her. They crowd round Duncan, who is raving about Canada. The lush forests! The open spaces! The generosity of the people! The exotic wildlife! Banff! Jasper! The salads! A Canadian knows how to make a salad! The mountain flowers. A spectacular country! *The* place to be. Forget London. New York. There's Toronto. Vancouver. The opportunities! His niece and nephew should move *at once* if they want to get ahead. Why let England hold them back?

"Our neighbour is still an asshole," the sister says, swinging on Roslyn. "Came over bangin' on the front door two in the mornin'. 'Turn down the goddamn music!' didn' he holler. An' I said, Charlie!" up shoots her thumb, "Crank 'er up!"

The sister never speaks to Roslyn again, not even when Roslyn says goodbye, but she stuffs a damp Beverley Horse Races pamphlet into Roslyn's hand. Roslyn opens it back at the hotel. Inside, in bold: *ARE YOU READY TO BE LUCKY?*

Next morning, after a dingy pub breakfast of eggs, half-cooked bacon, stewed tomatoes, braised mushrooms, a plop of pork and beans, and gum-slicing toast, they board a small plane and step off in Alicante, Spain. A lumpy-bottomed woman whizzes past the luggage carousel, hands flapping, breasts spilling out of a too-tight bra whose red back-clasp shows in the V of her sundress and gives her back-boobs. "I just put it down for a minute! I just set it down —"

"Woman! You left it on the plane!"

"Well, it's your bloody fault, it is."

Duncan's neck cranks at every bleached blonde with a bob.

"You're looking for Harriet!" Roslyn says.

"Don't be daft." Duncan lurches their rental car out of the parking stall, clatters over a flowerpot, pretends he didn't, and away they jolt. Ride-a-cock-horse. The Spanish house they've bought was only partially built on the day of sale, but the builder has promised it ready April fifteenth — yesterday.

"We're home!" Duncan beams. "Off to our villa!" Takes a wrong turn and sails them through the airport again. He and Harriet were in Spain once, twenty-six years ago, for seven days. To hear Duncan tell it, their sight-seeing moved between the pool and the pub. Duncan, never having driven a standard, whiplashes Roslyn out into the Costa Blanca landscape.

No oven blast heat today. Barely ten degrees. "It's freezing!" Roslyn says. A cold snap, Duncan grudgingly admits. Unusual. But he's sure the sun *will* shine. Mountains rise like mirages out of the cracked red earth. Duncan bobs them round a roundabout, nearly shaving the fender off a car — steering wheel on the wrong side — that zips across their lane and off the exit ramp. Duncan bucks down the ramp in its wake, the driver punching his fist in the air in some kind of angry swirl that looks obscene. "Europeans are aggressive," Duncan explains. "Canadians don't —"

"Duncan! You're on the wrong side of the road! Get *over!!!*"

Duncan cranks the wheel out of oncoming traffic. "No, I wasn't!"

They skim down the N332 toward San Fulgencio's *urbanización*. Oh my. The landscape! Not what Roslyn expected. Scrubby swampy brown. Cranes. So many building cranes. Where are the palm trees? Garbage whirls off building sites, Duncan whistling jauntily to show he's not bothered when a plastic sheet twines itself round their antenna. Three flamingos rise from a hot-pink pond. Salt beds sparkle like huge mounds of crushed ice.

Thirty minutes of this, and Duncan steers off another roundabout into La Marina of San Fulgencio. Roslyn catches a shimmering glimpse of the Mediterranean. "The sea! We'll go there every day!" Duncan promises; but already it's disappeared, and they are driving a narrow road flanked by tall dry grasses like old movies of Mexico. Duncan finds the main street after the second try, jounces down a steep hill, right, and right again, and pulls up in front of the *piso piloto* where he was directed in their correspondence to retrieve their keys. Yellow. Every house is yellow. Extremely yellow. There is Roslyn and Duncan's — hard to pick out except that many climbing the embankment are only partially built. Moroccan-looking. Small. Very small. Not villa-ish at all. So yellow. So high. So narrow. Barely six hundred square feet.

"It will be more spacious than it looks. And here! There's room for an underbuild!" Duncan says. "Don't worry! I've looked after everything. I've arranged the bed and sofa delivery from a local store. Our shipped goods should arrive within the week." They climb the tiled steps and look out across the dry ravine to the thin green watermelon-rind of sea. Long front windows open to the view. Duncan unlocks the triple-bolt front door.

Plaster dust flours the floor. Stucco-swirled walls. Missing baseboards. Wires hanging from the ceiling. Roslyn turns to Duncan, braced for the barrage. But he just says, "Bloody hell. We'll write a snag list."

"A what?"

"A list! You'll learn." He lets the door swing shut. "Of what wants fixing. No use cleaning until they finish off the work! You have to coddle workers here," he adds. "Praise their work. It makes them want to jump the queue, get to your list first. Watch me and follow; I'll show you how things are done."

Out the back bedroom windows, clumps of identical high thin houses rise up from building sites, as if filmed through a concave lens, dust-scarred, with staring holes for windows. A woman lolls on a chair in an open doorway. Across the alley, two men fist fight on a porch. Another woman steps out of her house in high heels and flings a bucket of water down her steps with ferocity.

Roslyn sets her suitcases on the bed, which gives up a poof of dust, and suggests wandering out for a bite. Together they climb the stiff ascent to the main street where Duncan is delighted to find a little bodega advertising, in English, "Pork chop and chips and mushy peas, tea included." Sounds-around English. British English. Every imaginable accent. Duncan scans the blondes.

"Don't bother yourself to tell her," the woman at the next table says to a man Roslyn guesses is her adult son. "Next time she can step out on her own." A green herb sticks to her lip. She turns to her husband. "You never trait me right!" And when he doesn't answer: "You're just going to sit there, aren't you! It's all you ever do!"

"I got you your sodding apple crumble."

They are all three stuffed into too-tight plaid shorts, sandals, and socks.

Roslyn digs for the camera, adjusting the focus past Duncan's head. Sets it on video. "Duncan Bloxham, in the fashion-forward mecca of San Fulgencio!"

"Not here!" Duncan hisses, grabbing at the camera, hand over the lens.

"Well, where then?"

"At the beach! Will you have pudding? We'll go to the beach tomorrow once we buy the garden furniture and beach towels and a beach umbrella. And the telly, of course. Sod off! Put the camera away!"

The woman scrapes up the last of her sodding apple crumble while the son and his father stare at the table leg as if expecting a magic trick. She swallows, stands, strides out the door and down the sidewalk. The son and father rise and amble behind, single file. Roslyn reaches for their abandoned newspaper. The *Costa Blanca News:* Cork Talk, Gadget Guru, The British Scene. She smoothes the paper closed. Reads aloud the front-page headline.

Land Grab Scams

More than 700 British residents took part in a noisy protest march to prevent the authorities from bulldozing eight homes — all of which had building licences revoked by the Junta. Carrying placards and loudhailers, protesters chanted in both English and Spanish: 'Right the injustice!' and *'Justicia sí, abusos no'.*

"Duncan! What the hell?" Roslyn reads on.

The owners of newly-constructed houses built on illegal land have been served with warrants that give them thirty days until their houses will be bulldozed. The owners will be charged for the cost of the bulldozing."

"People make stuff up," Duncan says, short laugh for effect, tapping his manicured nails against the table. "Christ. Put the paper away. Relax! We're in Spain!"

A man at an adjoining table says, "Mate a mine had watch and ring nabbed Sunday past, stopped to pay toll on motorway. Motorcyclist whipped between car and tollbooth and ripped jewellery right off 'im. In 'ospital, 'e is, cracked wrist, broken finger. Figures bloke on motorcycle pegged 'im and the missus when they stopped miles back for tea."

Duncan hops from foot to foot, complaining with a kind

of frantic cheerfulness of a sore back. Insisting Roslyn choose a "pudding." Why not try the brandy snaps?

Roslyn turns the page.

In Torrevieja, a karaoke singer was attacked by four women who disliked her performance.

"Let's get the telly," Duncan downs his Bustard Ale. "Wives' tales. Forget pudding. Let's get things in order."

When Roslyn and Duncan return from the far side of town, a man across the street in the house covered in blue decals and tea saucers, steps out, turns on a water hose, and sprays down a parrot sitting on the back of a deck chair. The bird spreads its feathers, clucking and squawking.

Duncan wrestles the TV out of the trunk while Roslyn hauls bags from the back seat. Through the back window she sees a grisly sea captain–type, shoulders wide as a trolley, oily rag in hand, pass on the pavement. "Sure you 'ave electric? Yer in Spain, mate," the man giggles. "*Mañana. Mañana.*"

The man with the water hose lays it aside, opens his gate, steps across, and is nearly clipped by a car roaring backwards up the street.

"You don't want nothin' to do with 'im." The parrot man nods at the retreating shoulders. Duncan grunts, hauling the television up the stairs. Parrot man turns to Roslyn. "That there's Bert," the man continues. "Lives in 30 with 'is girlfriend Nell. Edith in 31? One with the arse on 'er? Well, aren't she and Bert havin' a right go at each other."

He wipes his wet hands on his shorts. "Bert edges his bonnet just past Edith's gate, won't back 'er up for nothin'." He settles in against their rental car as if thinking of staying. "That meek little 'usband av 'ers don't say a word. Don't you just 'ate a man like that?"

A small white truck rumbles up. Out hops a Spaniard with a toothy smile and a big belly covered in white dust. He shakes parrot man's hand.

"Vasco!" the neighbour says. He turns to Roslyn. "Vasco 'ere's our builder, responsible for these 'ere fifty-two houses." His gesture takes in the half-built ones up the hill. Vasco, grinning, offers Roslyn his hand.

"You've done a beautiful job," Roslyn says. "*Usted se ve bueno!*" Vasco arrests mid-handshake, but hangs on, so Roslyn adds haltingly, "*Parece bueno.*" She studied Spanish online an hour a day their last thirty days in Canada. She's taught Duncan all she knows. Duncan's face appears over the porch rail. "*Parece MUY bueno!*" he calls down enthusiastically.

"*Gracias!*" Vasco chuckles. "*Muchas gracias!*" He nods up at Duncan, eyes turquoise sparklers. "Your husband *también?*" He coughs. Erupts in laughter. "So, *señorita.*" Both hands enclose Roslyn's. "On thees lawv-ley Mundi, you theenk I lewk gewd for sex? *Verdad?* I lewk gewd for sex? I think *tal vez* you wish say: *Su trabajo parece bueno!*" He bursts into guffaws. "Oh no?" Wipes his eyes. "*Quizà* I lewk gewd for sex!" He leans in. "You also, *señorita! Usted también!*"

A red-faced Duncan disappears behind the porch rail.

Duncan is fiddling with wires behind the television when Roslyn comes chortling up the stairs. "You told him he looked *really* good for sex!" She falls, giggling, onto the couch.

"Don't go around talking to men you don't know!" Duncan snaps. "That's not on! You do NOT talk to strange men!"

"Well, I can't talk to you then."

Duncan throws up his arms. "Ahhhhh!" The telly blurts to life and he slumps down onto the sofa, refusing to look at her, pouring himself *rioja* to the brim in a plastic cup he brought up from the car.

Late evening. Roslyn jogs out into the chill Spanish night, Duncan still parked in front of the blaring television, head bobbing against the sofa arm, emitting an occasional mournful wheeze, though he did jolt awake and flap her a weak, forgiving wave as she pulled the door shut behind her. She feels flush with energized goodwill. Heads along Calle San Sebastián. The ravine is a gaping sensual mouth between her and the Mediterranean. She picks up speed. She'll help him through. White houses shimmy down a distant hill. The moon looks second-hand, grey-green, as if a piece has broken off and is floating away. She skims along Calle San Sebastián to the cicadas' shrieking chorus. Hint of hibiscus, orange and lemon, weeds and ashes. Across the ravine, the ink-bleed of the sea. The air is damp. Roslyn passes a glow-worm, lit from within, clinging neon-greenly to a concrete wall. She lets go her clutch of unwritten postcards, lets go the winter sun burning a cold hole in her chest, lets go of the silver world they've left so far behind. Her feet scatter the bleached white stones of San Fulgencio.

And from nowhere, the rain. Rain like blisters. Small, sensuous punctures. Down a back alley, a peacock, blue-green as sea brume, plays percussion over broken bottles, grips the earth, dancing himself horny.

Roslyn lifts bare arms to the deluge. Baby. She is ready!

The
Costa Blanca
News

———

Uno

White lizards scrabble. Spanish sun plunges from a blood-scraped sky. San Fulgencio's burnt-fish air. Bird of paradise rusts on tiled porch steps, myrtle-seed, rosemary, olive and *níspero*. Waft of chips and mushy peas. The Mediterranean, reeking of corroded iron, whacks its shores like the snap of a dishrag. Two dogs fuck in a stony garden.

Dos

Here comes Nell stepping out a doorway, clutching Boodles British Gin in a brown paper sack. Well, she might be struck with the urge to drink. Bert might be struck with the urge to stop. What a dust-up would ensue! Their urges rarely intersect. Some of Bert's are a wee bit smutty. Word is he snogged a Spanish barmaid at the Gun and Giblets Tuesday past. Off with me mates, Bert likes to say. *Off with his head,* thinks Nell.

Nell locks Mavis's heavy front door, balancing in one arm her macaroni-cheese that was warming itself in Mavis's cooker, gin bottle clinking the baking platter, her wooden beads tangling with her Spanish cross, a near-nude Jesus clutching his perch. *What's wrong with you today, Nell?! Pull yourself together!*

Nell imagines the news of Bert's latest snog pulsing up Calle San Sebastián, through Doin' Your Head In where tutting foreign ladies smoke white trails over *Chat* and *OK!*, heads tin-foiled in *reflejos*, lacquer clasping at dried-out curls. *Get stuffed!* Nell tells those nosy parkers as she climbs Slim and Mavis's outdoor stairs to their rooftop patio. A patch of Mediterranean slices into view like a migraine across the red-baked ravine, sloshing water washing up debris. Nell's thigh muscles tremble, her knee near collapse.

Tres

"Did ya lock me front door?" Mavis hollers past the ruckus of Slim and Bert setting up the barbie, her head on fire with raspberry hair dye. "Did ya collect me cutlery?"

Nell waves the clinking forks and knives. Mavis, lolling in her garden chair, leans over her bulbous stomach to send Nell a thumbs up and a buck-toothed grin, wine carton teetering on the rooftop wall.

Ping! A zinging shot! Out dashes Bert from behind the potted kumquat tree, deking right, left, right in a running crouch, crisscrossing the sun-broiled tiles. "Pegged 'er!" he cries, and a yowling pussycat streaks the hot pavement below. Ping! Ping! Ping! Bert nails another. He's bowlegged, cocky, elated, prowling, a Viking, aiming his BB gun through Slim and Mavis's yellow turrets.

Bert and wild cats — don't even ask.

Cuatro

Nell watches Bert, and the gossip gathers like *gota fria* raindrops riding the levanter. *Bert Broadbent were fooling with a guapa barmaid.* The words, machine-gun fire gattling in Nell's head. They lift and sail right off the rooftop, straight for the *Caprabo,* where bikini-bulged foreigners with caking lipstick slap the aisles in silver flip-flops, pushing wonky carts past Spanish clerks, past rows of olives, past the fresh fish counter, where tilapia pant on icy shards, pin teeth clenched in disbelief. Idle ladies with dried-jerky skin, craving crème fraîche, chocolate bickies, and news. *Bertie Broadbent snogged Esperenza Oliveras,* who's under thirty if she's a day. Bert's pushing seventy, just one of the blokes who lurch the streets of this English enclave in *Bella España.* To pub for football, to pub for bingo, to pub for snooker. For a bit o' skirt. "For a bit o' fluff," Bert likes to say. Spanish girls tasty as a boiled sweet. "Off for a pint! 'Ave to 'ave me bitter," Bert cries every evening after five o'clock tea. Randy Bert on a rub dub shoney, while in their rabbit-hutch villa Nell grits her crooked teeth. Bert sliding crusty feet into heel-chomped sandals, grinning like a plonker, a tom in heat.

Cinco

A long-beaked bald ibis sails the oil-glazed sky like a ripped-off slice of floating canvas. Evening sticky with recycled heat. *Rojo* lilies swell and burn. Plácido Domingo from a CD player. Treacle and sponge dry in a microwave. Wind snatches dust from the olive boughs. A bone-thin donkey brays his thirst.

Seis

"Nell! You're gettin' fat!" Bert waves his cheap wine. Picks it up by the gallon behind the hairdresser shop. The wind whaps his words about the rooftop. "Park your fat arse here beside me, Nell!" Bert pats a sagging garden chair and over limps Nell. There she sits, addicted to disaster.

"Don't she look comfy balanced on her bulging backside!" Bert's giggles snip the air like pinking shears.

"Well, crikey, who's this?" Bert does a double take as two heads pop up over the stair wall: a woman shimmering in a sunburst sundress. It hurts Nell's eyes. Bert's face lights like a sky on fire. Flat stomach, tiny breasts, shiny shoulders. A silver-haired man, one step behind, in an avocado dress shirt. "Decoration for the party! Who's this smart set?" cries a flush-faced Bert. Slim does introductions. He met the two at market just this morning: Duncan Bloxham, and Roslyn, his American wife.

"Canadian," the woman says, hair mangled by the wind.

"Same thing," Bert says. He whistles, "Wacko!"

"Hiya!" says Mavis. "How long ya been here?"

"Almost a month!" the Canadian says. "We've been

taking day trips up country — Elche, Guadalest, Alcoy, Valencia. Next we're heading to Barcelona. Has anyone holidayed in the interior? We saw these adorable little roe deer!"

"Ya must be mistaken. No deer in Spain," Slim says. "Just cats," and everybody laughs.

"No! There were! Little deer in the ditches. We ended up on this gravel road —" A blast of hot wind makes the rooftop shudder, flattening the woman's hair into a bullet-shaped cone.

"Ya got everything you want right here," Mavis says into the sudden silence.

"Of course! Of course!" says Duncan Bloxham, hand clamped tight on his wife's shoulder. "We're here for the beaches. Who wouldn't be?"

But Bert's already bragging, all the places he has plans to go. News to Nell: haven't they been in Spain nine months, and can Nell pry the man off the sodding sofa to drive to Almoradi market, fifteen minutes down the road?

While Bert paces the rooftop, strutting and preening, Mavis peers at Nell's cellulite and bruises poking out her walking shorts. "What's 'appened to ya this time?"

"*Eres guapa!*" Grinning at the Canadian, Bert slaps his thigh. Winky jumps and piddles. Dismal Winky, back end dragging, startled from his sad funk, yapping crazily.

"Crikey, Slim! Ya mucky bugger! Don't swipe up the piddle with me indoor mop!" Mavis leaps up to give the tiles a good wash, one more push-through before the barbie gets going.

"What 'appened to Nell?" Bert leans and flicks her neck, voice alive with flirtation and wine. "Slipped in the shower scrubbing herself down. Don't she walk now with a rod up her arse! I'm left to haul the woman mornings out a the bath."

The Canadian, startled, turns toward Nell, her satiny dress so new and shiny, Nell expects a price tag attached under the arm. The woman's dressed for a destination wedding.

"Tell us 'bout Canada!" Mavis says.

"It's bloody winter all year long," Duncan Bloxham undoes a button on his avocado dress shirt. Slim and Bert circling in their rumpled T's.

"Duncan! It is *not!* Don't make up stories! Our Chinooks can make it warmer than winters here in Sp —"

"Ain't she a wee thing!" Bert elbows Slim, grinning.

Duncan Bloxham's chin juts; he begins fast-talking. "Quaint bunch, Canadians, striding off on walks. Minute we unpacked here, didn't Roslyn dart away!" His face morphs for a moment into a squinting bulldog's. He chug-a-lugs the beer Slim hands him. "I don't know where she goes, well I don't, then, do I? I haven't a bloody clue!"

"You won't want to be walking here on the Costa Blanca," Mavis pops an olive behind her teeth. "Obviously. A fast tramp on a winter day is one thing altogether. But march in this heat? You'd have to be daft! Hits a hundred ten degree! Well, it do, don' it."

The Canadian takes a slow stroll around the rooftop, as if to show them how it's done, feigning interest in Mavis's potted flowers.

Bert says, "Tell you what, I'd whisk 'er into the *Verde!*" crying after her how fond he is of exercise. "I own me a second house, far edge of town. If ya find yourself wantin' to head in me direction . . ." He giggles soundlessly, winks at

Nell, and eats up the woman with waggle-wolf eyes. Duncan Bloxham downs two more beer.

"Bert!" Nell grinds her teeth, necklace swinging; Jesus turns a somersault and grimly grips his cross. "The only walk you manage beelines straight to pub!"

"Oh, right," says Mavis, "isn't Bert at 'er again."

Bert giggles, "Well, who can blame a bloke for tryin'? This lovely lady here 'as a fine set a *labios!*"

The Canadian's face fills fast with colour, like a sponge sucking in red wine. Duncan swings round on Bert as he and Slim explode in laughter; Duncan changes his mind, and chuckles along. Joke's on the couple! "Haha! No harm done!" Slim chortles, gasping, bent over his belly. A white bird runs past him on the rooftop wall. Mavis explains: *labios* is "lips" in Spanish. Another good laugh and drinks all round. Mavis asks opinions about her poinsettia, a scarlet slash against the orange kumquat.

Duncan points out that the colours clash. Mavis stares him down with her bulgy eyes.

After the barbie — Nell smells blood sausage — they'll play *Who Wants to Be a Millionnaire.* Mavis is barmy for the game. Makes Slim play to get his supper.

May heat slides across the rooftop, turning the tiles into iridescent streaks. Bert, happily cabbaged, goofily grinning, nudges in beside the Canadian. Propped on a garden chair, he fiddles with a crusty toenail. "Me son lived in Canada a few years back."

Duncan Bloxham peers over the rooftop, staring gloomily out to the splinter of sea, now and then turning to slit-eye his wife and throw his head about like an angry horse.

"Place called Jasper. Worked as a ski bum."

Duncan says, "The wild animals there are someth —"

"Jasper!" the woman cries. "That's right near my home!"

Duncan stares at his wife as if she were a telly made of snowy dots and he's trying to focus. "Ex*cuse* me, I believe that *I* was speaking? Jasper near Calgary? Not at all. It's six sodding hours' drive! Canadians wander cross the country just for tea."

"We went wandering last night. Parked the caravan down by the sea. Din' we Nell? Karaoke on the beach. Got the idea over pork patties for tea. Had to see that bloke from Benidorm, what does Rod Stewart so well."

"Bert were having such a time, he clean forgot the caravan."

"Topless beach." Bert cups his hands under his armpits.

"I guess that makes sense." Slim yanks down his fedora sitting on his head like a Spanish gangster's.

"Tits pulled up to their ears, just the way I Iike 'em."

Slim and Bert and Duncan drink to that. The Canadian tucks her arms in, twists one foot around her ankle, turning herself into a human twizzle.

"Well, you did, didn' you, Bert?"

"Did what, Nell?"

"Clean forgot. Bert trotting 'cross a field three in the mornin' —"

"Hurtling after me, the woman were, over globs a donkey shite an' clumps of dirt, trying to get me to turn around."

"When Bert wouldn', I let me handbag fly —"

"Clipped me on me ear, sent me glasses sailing."

"I thought there were something different, Bert." Slim

runs fat fingers over sunburned ears. "Hear ETA's set off another bomb. Spanish can't control themselves. Too much hysterics. Check the sausage."

"The Spanish're like thread through a needle." Mavis weaves over to the spitting barbie. Slim and Bert and Duncan drink to Spanish passion.

"Spectacles. Obviously. That's what's missing." Mavis glugs wine straight from the cardboard carton.

"There we was in the cack-brown field down on our knees in pitch black, no moon, pawing about the lumpy earth. And din' Nell go and step on me spectacles! I've had to send to England for different pair!" Tonight Bert's drinking double. Can't see anyway.

"Right. Well, just t'other day," Mavis waves her carton, "weren't I forced to club a cabbie with me Burberry handbag? One of them foreign turbaned fellows. Couldn't follow directions tied to 'is earlobe."

Siete

Nell's bloody knackered. Why's she even here? Left thigh screaming.

"Sent an invite to seven couples." Mavis into a story Nell's already heard. "By Saturday mornin' hadn't everybody fallen out. First there were Alice come by Tuesday where I were ironing down in me garage, cigarette smoking. Stopped to remark I put her in mind of a washerwoman, always cleaning me stairs and doin' other people's ironing. Did ya ever! This after Alice got herself a sprained wrist and talked me into laundering four sets av her curtains."

Slim says, "Ya is forever scrubbing down the stairs."

"Oh right. Fast as our piddling Winky refouls them! To say nothing of cat pee and sand-rains!" Mavis spills wine and sops it up. "Then Wednesday afternoon Edith and Charlie borrowed our auto. Ran straight into light pole, din' they, Slim? Heading for Almoradi market. Who needs Almoradi? We 'av market up the street! Put 'em right off when we says, Repair it. Liz's not on speaking terms (and Vinny supports her) on account a how, when I had me nails done, I invited Mary Crawford, just arrived in Spain. Well, I had me reasons! Obviously. Then didn't me and Mary end up in a row over at Torrevieja bingo hall. Do ya play bingo?" Mavis asks the Canadian.

"Folk in Canada don't play bingo."

"Of course they do, Duncan! Lots of people do! Just because I don't—"

Duncan gestures with his beer. "Ladies and gentlemen, I stand corrected."

"Keep 'er speakin'!" Bert's still grinning. "Smashing, way she clips 'er words!"

Nell says, "It's because she don't speak English. No — what she speaks ain't English. Well, she speaks Canadian!"

"Whatever the wee thing speaks, let's hear more av it! You been to the Chinese? In Guardamar? Smashing menu. We'll take you, the weekend, won't we Nell? You'll be wanting to order: E, G, and O."

Nell sits like a plug on her bulging bottom. Mavis told her yesterday, since nobody were coming, forget the fancy dress party, which put Nell off as what's she — nobody? But she kept mum and now she's planted on Mavis's garden chair, nerve pain scratching, next to the Canadian, shining in her dress like a copper penny.

Ocho

A baby yowls on the street below.

"Confound that noisebox!" Mavis says. "The tot's irritating as Edith's wind chimes. The child belongs to that gold digger what stole June's husband at the New Year dance. Not to be racialist but the woman's part Japanese. Lives one down from the German who don't speak to no one. That there's Snake, his Rottweiler, stiff with dirt." Mavis points with her hat, snatched off the table, at the mum hopping about beneath her bottle brush tree, the soccer-ball baby hunched in its pushchair, orange blossom ears, gumming on a sour soother.

The grimacing baby keeps its eyes fixed on Snake, dolefully loping about the courtyard, on three legs since the Kraut ran him over.

"The mum cuts hair to make a penny. She's the one what come from Manchester." Mavis splashes a slurp of wine across the sausage. The barbie flames up. Bert applauds.

Nell says, "She's the one what come to cut Bert's hair."

Bert giggles.

"Oh Bert!" says Mavis.

"Oh Bert!" Slim says, grinning like a carp.

"Didn' I walk in," Nell grips her Boodles British, "and catch that tart letting Bert cop a feel. Who knows how far things might have transgressed if I hadn't returned from market and happened in upon 'er."

Slim gives Bert's arm a sympathetic squeeze.

"Nell here's been wanting Spanish lessons —"

"Me too!" the Canadian enthuses.

"You don't need 'em, do you?" cries Bert. "Ain't much point to it in the end. Nell, fetch over the pitcher would you? My wine here 'as 'most disappeared."

Nell limps to the table and pours Bert wine. Sitting back down takes longer than rising.

"Who runs into the Spanish anyhoo?" Mavis holds her glass out. "Obviously."

So up gets Nell and does it all again, tripping over Winky, who's trying to catch the dribbles.

"They're daft, the Spanish," Bert waves an airy hand. "Daft as a hairbrush. Can't even think. Say things like, 'The Mrs. Rossi'. A barmy lot. Can't be taken serious. And wouldn't you know it, Nell's been wanting to drive. The woman don't even know where to go, does she!"

A sudden swarm of African bees zooms the rooftop, lands on the wisteria, and skids back into the milky evening sky.

"Shut up, Bert." Nell twitches a needle-cramp out of her gam. "You're the one what had three accidents in Wakefield."

Bert empties his glass, scarfs a swig of Nell's gin.

"Did you check the sausage?" Slim asks Mavis.

"Well one were the result of having to pick you up at bingo, wern' it. I were driving along and din' a woman back right into me!"

"No, Bert she didn'. You ran into her. And I were taking your mother to bingo night at the Veteran's Hall because you couldn't be bothered."

"Don't you like a feisty woman?" Bert giggles, his foot see-sawing. "How about a bit of a fumble when we get home, Nell? We haven't had a fumble in a donkey's age. Got to see if old George here can still salute!"

"More firewater for the natives." Mavis weaves down the stairs to fetch more spirits.

Duncan is leaning against the rooftop wall, explaining the American stock market; nobody's listening.

"Now there's a sexy woman!" Bert cries, jauntily stepping up to lean beside Duncan. High-heeled shoes and lacy skirt snapping up Calle San Sebastián.

"You have yourself a sexy woman, Bert." Mavis winks at Nell, who gives Jesus a sassy swing.

"Am I sexy then, Bert?" Nell asks slyly.

"No, Nell," Bert tells her. "You ain't."

Nueve

The levanter whistles round the chimney. Gritty sea sand bites the wind, hoisting the prim skirts of a startled nun's habit. Praying mantis wavers on bottle-green stick-legs; an angry strand of saffron sticks to a fork.

Diez

Nell stares at Bert's beer gut sloped like the sled-run she saw through a winter storm in Jasper, Canada. Out behind a church, kids yahooing in woollen balaclavas like escaping bandits, hurtling from the snow. Bert's grandchildren—son married a Canadian—let out head-banging screeches if they don't get their way, which, when Nell and Bert visit, they make sure is often. Have to show a youngster who's in charge. Can't leave the table till you've downed your cereal. Sure it's soggy. We don't give a toss. One morning the girl refused to pull on her knickers. Wanted the purple pair, wouldn't touch the white. Nell held her down and stuffed her legs through. Kicked in the ear, she was, for her efforts. And didn' the bloomin' wife show them the door. Cheeky! What were they? Hired help? Nell were glad to go, and she bloody well said so, fed up with painting the stairwell mould-green, fed up with babysitting while the son and wife came in the door, fast, every evening, and raced to the cellar to ride off wildly on stationary bicycles. What the blither? Also ready to lop off Bert's head for disappearing to pub, staggering home at all hours, bragging how Canadian girls love a British accent.

Once

The sausage is ready. The mozzies are circling.

"Mavis, your jumper is arse-about!" Slim drags it up her arms, catching her heaving bosoms, and yanks it about so it's facing forward.

"Blimey," Mavis yelps, staring at her bare arms, "if I ain't wearing two watches! Clean forgot I had on t'other. One set for London. One for La Marina!"

Nell doesn't need a watch. Time slowed to a halt the day she packed her bags and moved to paradise with Bert. She touches her eye beneath her sunglasses, the sore spot a miniature cushion of pins.

"Where's the tin opener?" Mavis down on her knees in

her jogging bottoms, knickers sticking out the top. "Pine-apple slice wants opening."

"You nick it, Slim? Need the tin opener to prise your woman's legs?" Bert nudges Duncan, grinning at Duncan's wife.

"Rhubarb and rubbish!" Mavis hauls to her feet. "Sod off, ya prat." They get in a friendly slinging match, Mavis and Bert, that ends in an arm tussle, Bert clasping Mavis sideways, groping her boobs, her hair exclaiming redly to the sky. Mavis, chuffing, untangles, gives Bert a swat, and retrieves the opener from under her own chair.

"Just like a woman," Bert gasps, giggling. "Park on 'er and squawk."

Blood sausage, cauliflower, jacket potatoes. And Nell's dried-out macaroni-cheese, which nobody touches except the Canadian. Everyone perspiring into their food, forking in chunks of sausage and mushy peas, while the evening wind sashays about the rooftop, rummaging rudely in Nell's ears. The blamed levanter won't leave her alone. Blowing at her pinched nerves, broken bones, stomach troubles. What could come to lighten her mood? American crime stories. Tonight, while Bert snores, she'll watch *CSI: Miami*.

Doce

Bert clatters his plate down. "Your key! Your key!" he hollers to Mavis. "I need the loo pronto!" Winky makes short work of Bert's spill, gulping and lapping with his lewd tongue.

Mavis fishes her keys from her shirt pocket.

"Have to keep doors locked," Slim explains to Duncan.

"Can't trust Romanians. Can't trust Spanish. Can't even trust the burgling Brits. You can't do 'er at home?" he calls after Bert. "You're but three doors down!"

Slim's holler is for nothing. Bert pounding down the stairs. "Now's not the moment to prat about! Outa me way. I'm 'bout to blow!"

"Got enough loo rolls?" Nell asks Mavis. "Bert takes big dumps." She kicks a cauliflower sliver stuck to her toe. "Flush in the middle!" she calls down the stairwell. "You won't be wanting a back up, Slim."

Nell takes the opportunity to describe Bert's dumps: humungous, wide-weighted turds of porridgy texture.

The Canadian looks in need of a drink.

"Bert's dumps are a right problem for ya then." Slim scrapes burnt sausage off the barbie.

"Well, it's me what takes the plunger, innit, each time that Bert plugs the loo. Mostly Bert's blows're the result a take-away. But gherkins are the culprit número uno."

Mavis found the gherkins on offer at the Mercadona. "Two euro sixty if you buy two jar."

The three take a tally of what makes people blow. Greasy. Fried. Spicy. Raw fruit and corn.

Duncan Bloxham has three beers in quick succession while Slim shares what he read in a barber-shop maga-zine: when a group of people gather, as in caravan camping, magically their dumps coincide.

"You're speakin' out yer arse," scoffs Mavis. "That's not dumps, that's woman's menstruation. A flamin' embarrass-ment, being married to a plonker who don't know his bol-locks from his elbow!"

"What's for pudding?" a flushed Slim growls.

"Choc-ice and bickies. And these Spanish pastries dusted with powdered sugar what catches in the throat and makes a bloke cough. Eat 'er up," Mavis says, "and on with the game."

Slim lights a smoke. "Who'll be having tea?"

The Canadian takes another turn about the rooftop, face disappeared in the potted calla lilies. Duncan Bloxham glowers in her general direction.

They're finishing pudding when Bert pops back up the stairwell.

"Good dump?" Slim asks.

"Oh boy, were she." Bert drops, sweaty-faced, and does seven press-ups. "Come sit by me, Nell." And over Nell limps.

"Taken her to doctor?" Mavis, eying Nell's walk.

"Woman won't make her mind up, I can't be bothered. Can't be doin' with that."

"With what?"

"The sick! With cripples! Can't be running after someone who won't get out of bed. I'm busy afternoons — motorcycle races on the telly. Fetch a cup of tea, maybe, but that's the extent av it."

"Send yer bloke back to England. That's what ya do," Mavis mutters to Nell, yanking the computer out of its case.

"Go easy!" Slim snarls.

"Bert can't go back," says Nell. "Shot at in 'is car. The Jag with the window what won't unroll. Had our front door kicked in one morning in Wakefield. Didn' change up registration when he bought the vehicle."

"I did do," says Bert, biting into a biscuit.

"They believe he's the loan shark what last owned the car."

"When were this, Bert?"

"Three girlfriends back."

"So you can't return to England?"

"I might do," Bert says defiantly.

Mavis says, "Well, I'm goin' to England, see me a doctor. Leaving in a fortnight, an on-offer flight. The Spanish doc won't treat me unless I stop drinking."

"The cowboy!" Bert says.

"The tosser!" says Mavis.

"Nell's pap," Bert says, "is about to pop his clogs. Eighty-six year, and hangin' by a frayed thread. Nell jumps like a jackbox each time the telephone rings. Puts a fella off with her carryin' on. Crikey! Put a sock in it! I tell her. The man is decrepit, 'e's bound to kick the pot. Look what 'appens to Spanish women. Waist like a wasp when they're eighteen. Marry 'em off, and ten years in, what you got? Great moving squares with a head and legs. Well, look at Nell and we ain't even married! Woke up this morning," Bert waves his pudding spoon. "I were lying there, peaceful-like, goin' over in me head what I were going to do today, and Nell announces, 'It's our anniversary.' 'What anniversary?' I says. 'We ain't even married.' 'Twelve year to the day,' says Nell, 'since I moved in.' Now din't that go and spoil me think! Nell coming up with a notion like that." The Canadian rises, set her plate on the table. Bert leans over, gives her bottom a pinch.

"Bert, you *did* say we'd get married. Yes, Bert, you did! You said on the telephone! 'Why don' you move down to

Wakefield at month's end, get a part-time job and we'll get married.' I were thinking, Bert —"

"Oh, don't do that, Nell. You'll get yourself knackered."

"Well, anyways," says Mavis, pouring wine for all, "sod the Spanish. Who knows what they're saying with those unnatural lisps."

Slim shares that in a restaurant in Santa Pola the waiter brought him a cracked white bowl, nothing in it but a bit of broth and a humungous meatball covered in nuts.

"It's the Germans what are the nancy boys," says Bert. "Hogging beach chairs. Hogging public telephones. Sticking out their elbows, budging the queue. Weren't a week past at the Guardamar beach, din' I have to beat up a German for wearing white socks?"

Trece

Magenta sun plummets down a bloodshot sky.

"Time!" Mavis hits the button and the music swells. *Who Wants to Be a Millionaire?* Everyone scrapes chairs up to the computer except for Duncan, who is in a twilit corner, hanging, mouth agape, off the garden swing.

Which of the following is a road safety official? A. Wine gum woman; B. Lollipop lady; C. Bubblegum bloke; D. Gobstopper guy.

Mavis hits B. "Lollipop lady!"

"Blimey, woman!" Slim twists on his chair. "There's five of us what's playing the game!"

So far so good! chants the man on the screen. *Well done! You've earned one hundred pounds!*

The Anthem of West Ham United is "I'm forever blow-ing _____." Bert thinks it's "Over." Mavis pushes D. Bubbles.

"Don't hog the game, Mavis," Slim says warningly.

Spot on! Now for three hundred quid:

What breed of dog is also a type of undie? "Bloodhound," Bert says. "Boxer!" Mavis cries.

Already four hundred quid! You're working your way toward a thousand pounds!

Slim breathes through his nose. "Yer cabbaged," he hollers.

Duncan sits up fast, staring behind him, as if he fears the ravine out in the dark is moving closer. "Quiet!" he barks, head cocked, listening, before grasping his own wrist, and sinking back from view.

Moving right along! A set of photographs of known criminals is commonly called a rogues' _____. A. Gallery; B. Balcony; C. Terrace; D. Patio.

"Gallery!" Mavis yells and hits the A.

Well done! You have five hundred pounds!

"Mavis, will ya quit bein' the fookin' hotshot?"

Which of these is an offensive weapon? A. Finger pol-isher; B. Wrist wiper; C. Knuckle duster; D. Nail cleaner.

"Knuckle duster!" shouts Slim, stabbing C.

Spot on! Six hundred quid! Now for the double. You are going for twelve hundred! Are you ready?

"Do I love her? Does a fel-ler love pi-i-i-i-ie?" One hand appears above the swing back, beating time like a conductor's.

Who was the Greek goddess of love?

"Venus!" Bert says. "Won' I know? Venus!"

"Naw, Aphrodite," Mavis snorts.

"She's right, Aphrodite," the Canadian says. Slim shoves Mavis's hand out of the way. Hits B. Venus.

The music bongs flat. Awwww! Wrong answer. Game over! I'm afraid you go away with ab-so-lutely nothing!

"Brilliant!" Mavis swings on Slim. "Ain't ya a walkin' encyclopedia!"

"Piss off! You're bladdered, Mavis! Ya ruined it with yer showin' off!"

"Fancy Slim Walmsey! Man o' the match!"

Slim's face darkens to ripe aubergine. "Naff off!" He lunges, they skid along the table's edge, sweeping wine glasses crashing to the tiles, Slim's arms clenched round Mavis's elbows, Mavis flapping, slapping, blubbering, walloping at air. They stumble apart, and mash together, clothes pressed by wind, high-stepping over shattered glass.

The Canadian backs toward the garden swing, and wetting her lips, sinks tight beside her husband. His eyes snap open: two staring blood clots. "Blimey, Roslyn! Move yourself over! A man would appreciate *some* room."

Laughing Bert half-rising, pinching Nell's arm: "That's showing some fight, that is! You go, girl! Slim, she just might ding ya 'fore ya hit Round Two!" Bert's big-sandaled foot see-sawing the terrazzo floor. Mavis shrieking, "Bugger off, arse! Leave me *be!*" Slim wrenches her about; a quick grab; swings her.

Thunk! Her head hits the gazebo pole.

One strung hushed note. Mavis, sprawling slow motion toward the moon-green tiles. Cicadas resume shrieking in the trees below.

Slim heaves himself up, hands stuck with glass shards.

"Can't be doin' with you, woman. I'm 'eading ta pub!"

A grinning Bert hauling Nell from her garden chair. "Let's 'urry home, woman, take advantage! You're gonna get yer anniversary surprise. Collect your gin, girl. Yer gonna need 'er." Nell skids down the tiled stairs, Bert driving her forward.

Catorce

Salt skin. Dark stains. Wine-soaked tablecloth. Mavis teeters to her feet, pressing hands against the table. Hard lump of something underneath a serviette. Bert's forgotten BB gun. Mavis scrapes it out from the shattered glass, and reels down the darkened staircase.

Quince

The Canadian, eyes burning like they're leaking raw sewage, gathers plates and wipes up spills. Her husband staggers off the garden swing. "I feel a glow just thinking oooooof you!" His voice recedes down Calle San Sebastián.

A Canadian on a patio. Chopped-off like a half-finished sentence. Stifling scent of decaying hibiscus. Dank blood sausage smell of Mavis.

Silhouetted in an alley, a woman buys Ecstasy.

Light snuffs out at Bert and Nell's.

The water sloshing sloshing closer.

Crack! The Mediterranean fractures its shore.

Left

═══

The Scottish landscape skims by, bottle-green and soaking. They took the plane this morning from stifling Alicante to chilly Aberdeen, just three days after a quick trip to Canada to close the sale of Roslyn's house. She needs recuperation from their San Fulgencio neighbours, so Duncan arranged the hire car and here they are, driving up to New Pitsligo — a break from Spain's claustrophobic heat and Duncan's non-stop rounds fixing everyone's electric. Fancies himself *the man*, though not a single neighbour's paid him. An adventure this is going to be: see Duncan's old Aunt Midge in her slate cottage. His dead mother's sister. Duncan's told her the story. How his concerned mother moved up here from the north of England, four years before she died, to try to put things right with her sister, work out the inheritance. Roslyn's idea, this trip. Be a sport. Mend old rifts. She stood behind Duncan as he shouted into the phone box from the stone pub off the A950 carriageway. "Yes, but a stone's throw. Yes, we are a bit peckish. Yes, Sunday roast will be just dandy."

The first time Duncan asked her if she was feeling peck-ish, Roslyn thought he meant did she want sex. What a disappointment when he opened the freezer door and offered her a pop tart.

They haven't spoken for going on two hours. Not since Roslyn mentioned over the drumming on the rental car roof that all this rain is like the monsoons of Africa she saw on the Discovery Channel, and Duncan said it wasn't anything like Africa, nothing at all. *Aren't you something.* He nodded off in the passenger seat fifteen minutes ago, head bobbing forward. All that strain to win the war of silence has tuck-ered him out. Roslyn studies the back of Duncan's head, a smidgeon too flat above the puffy grey hairs flouffing out below the thinning. The overall effect: a bed skirt. But she's feeling magnanimous and perky here behind the wheel on the wrong side of the road. The British have so much to deal with: the price of petrol, bad teeth, quarrels, fallings-out as Duncan calls them — a two-hour silence is nothing. Duncan's mother and Aunt Midge said their last words in 1969. Twelve years later, Aunt Midge drove to the charity hospital and stood at the end of her sister's bed. A ward of seven women, one French and tied to her chair for trying to escape, face dolloped in plum-sized bruises, crying, "Untie me, *je vous en supplie!*" while Aunt Midge shifted in her walking shoes and watched her sister die. They stared each other down till Duncan's mother closed her eyes for good. *I win!*

"How do you know all this, Duncan?" Roslyn will ask after one of these stories.

"Aren't you perfect!" he'll reply. "Aren't you something."

Duncan and his sister who lives here haven't spoken in

going on seven years. Ever since the sister asked Duncan what he thought of her new garden furniture, and Duncan told her. Aunt Midge blames Duncan's mother for their youngest sister's death. "Well, it was his mother what bought her the ice cream at the fair, din' she then, and if Agnes din' take sick of scarlet fever within three days." "I *know*," Roslyn said to Stella when she first started hearing the stories. "The Brits! The Scots! They're crazy!" Add to that Uncle Potter's missing watches and you have an outright feud.

Roslyn glances at Duncan, hung forward against his seat belt as if on a county fair ride. If she slammed on the brakes his forehead would smack the dash. She doubts this is the beginning of The Silent Years. Duncan has so much yet to say. Take yesterday evening, during take-off from the Alicante airport. Roslyn, digging in her purse for gum, came upon two Kit Kat bars.

Roslyn: Do you want a chocolate bar, Duncan?

Duncan: (staring at her offering) Do you have one?

Roslyn: Here!

Duncan: That's not a chocolate bar. That's a biscuit.

Roslyn: I don't care what it's called. Do you want one? (By now both pinned against their seats, harder to fight, necks kinked as the lumbering Ryanair dragged itself sky-ward).

Duncan, fishing in his carry-on, pulled out two Penguins he'd been saving since he picked them up at The British Pantry in Calgary before they left for Spain. "Can't buy these in Canada unless they're imported," he told her for the umpteenth time. Chuckling. "The things that have to be imported in your country!" Things nobody but Duncan hankers after: crème fraîche, double cream, Mr. Kipling's Cherry Bakewell tarts. He undid the tiny tray attached to the seat in front, although the plane was still climbing, blocked as they were from the sightline of the flight attendants buckled in front and back. He arranged the chocolate bars — his, hers — for her to inspect.

Duncan: Now, you would call these chocolate bars, would you?

Roslyn: Yes, Duncan. I would.

Duncan: (triumphantly) Well, they're not! They're biscuits!

Roslyn: In England it's a biscuit. In Canada it's a chocolate bar!

Duncan, chuckling, tucked the bars away, shaking his head. Wasn't she cute.

Roslyn speeds up the windshield wipers and peers through the rain. How many years does she have left of Duncan's solicitous lectures? Don't people eventually get liver cancer drinking like he does? And why did these antics not irritate her until after the wedding? Sure, she saw his flaws, but she got lost in his elegant suits and ties, his showering of gifts. A Deepa Gurnani Odette Crystal Swirl Barrette. A Gucci handbag. Ruby earrings. A Fig Duo Latham and Neve pendant. Waterbridge Wine Gums (imported). Tunnock's Snowballs (imported). This was how much Duncan loved her. A fresh-cheeked Canadian thirteen years his junior who inherited good legs. Harriet's look like Olive Oyl's on the old Popeye cartoons. They have no calves. Roslyn's seen the pictures. There's Harriet, smiling, a pair of crutches disappearing up her skirt. During the divorce, Harriet threatened to cut up the sofa pillows. And she drove over her jewellery with the car.

"*Whose* jewellery?" Roslyn had said, hand stilled over the potatoes she was cutting for steak chips. Steak chips are thicker than other chips, Duncan has informed her. Eating thin ones with steak puts Duncan right off his food. "*Whose* jewellery? Her *own?*" Duncan gave her *the stare*, peeling mangos there beside her, the one fruit Roslyn is allergic to. She imagines he perfected *the stare* on Harriet: incredulity coupled with contempt, and a dob of exasperation. "Harriet is a remarkable mother!" Duncan said, brandishing the slippery mango, though one of his rules is Roslyn must not talk with her hands. If that mango touched Roslyn's skin, she'd be straight to the hospital. "You didn't even know Harriet!" Duncan's face clamped as if Roslyn were a bad smell. Of course she didn't know Harriet! Duncan remains outraged at Harriet's stashes of see-through underwear, price tags still dangling, that he found stuffed in the broom closet, in the breadbox, in the freezer behind the cheese, but if Roslyn dares to say a word against Spindle-Legs, the only way to make up for it is bake for a week. Duncan loves her baking, though he won't admit it. Where does he think she thinks it goes? On his third muffin, chuckling, "Ah, I see you're onto *muffins* this morning. Well, let's just eat *muffins* then. Ha. Thinking about *cookies* next? Heh heh." Lunging in for another when he thinks her back is turned. Cookies and muffins, he has informed her, are kiddies' food. So American! Good-natured chuckle. What does she know about baking anyway? Duncan's father *owned* a bakery.

Roslyn shifts behind the wheel and looks out at all those wet cows. The two of them are still jet-lagged from their jaunt to Canada. Jet lag wires her. It puts Duncan under, that and his assembly line of scotch on the rocks. "I can do it," Roslyn had said, getting behind the wheel after Duncan nearly puttered off the road. How much can there be to it? Position the car on the left side of the road and hit the gas.

Roslyn cranks the wheel toward a sudden exit off the thoroughfare at the New Pitsligo sign, jolting Duncan awake. "It's Pitsligo!" Roslyn says. Sure enough, they can see the roofs of the drenched village over a hill, Duncan's childhood home, well, where he lived the first three years of his childhood before his father abruptly moved the family to England. No, Duncan doesn't know why. Duncan sits up, rubs down his hair and shakes his head at her as if she has done something cheeky by steering the car here. The windshield wipers slap at the slashing rain and Duncan points out gloomily that they could be in forty-degree heat on a rooftop in Spain. Roslyn wonders why he gave in to her nudges to return to his roots. Perhaps fond memories of his mother. He has said he will visit her grave. Roslyn read out loud on the plane from the tourist information guide: Pitsligo was inhabited at the beginning of the present century by illicit distillers who presented a mean and miserable appearance, but, the guide assured the reader, all that has changed. It is now noted for its rock quarry and its present staple industry: the hand manufacture of bobbin lace.

Roslyn must remember not to dart about like a chicken with its head cut off inside Aunt Midge's cottage. Duncan is irked she moves so fast. Roslyn grew up on a Saskatchewan farm. Once a year her mild-mannered father organized the chopping block, an axe, pails of boiling water, and set about violently whacking chickens' heads off. And oh, the speed with which those headless birds hit the ground running, dizzy and listing, hightailing after Roslyn no matter which direction she sprinted in silent horror, zigzagging through the barnyard, neck cranked, broad-jumping cow pies — the chickens ran straight through, spurting blood out their headless holes — while back at the chopping block, the abandoned heads stared at each other from one beady astonished eye.

"Pits-*lag*-o. It's Pits-*lag*-o," Duncan enunciates as they careen the last mile down the carriageway. He's grown consistently more dreary and melancholic as the car lapped up the miles. He brought Harriet here twenty-six years ago, but she put everyone off with her toe ring and manicured fingernails, and if she told a story, they all just stared at her and said, "Oh . . . right."

It's up to Roslyn.

"There's no 'a'," Roslyn says. A semi hurtles by, rattling their rental car. "Pitsligo has two 'i's."

"Pits-*lag*-o," Duncan grinds out, swinging his body away from her. Swinging isn't easy in this little rental car.

Roslyn slows and they enter the grey wet village. Behind it rises the eastern slope of verdant Turlindie Hill.

"Idyllic!" Roslyn breathes.

"Twenty is plenty," Duncan says.

The New Pitsligo Bread and Biscuit Works looms suddenly on the right. Roslyn skids the car and sprays to a halt across the street from the old white stucco building. She takes deep breaths, feels like Toad in *The Wind in the Willows* behind the wheel of a motorcar. The same vicarious thrill she felt marrying elegant gloomy Duncan, until he began insisting on Spotted Dick for pudding, a dreadful spongy affair with dried fruit and currants, insisting she warm the plates for dinner, insisting Canadians are too attached to plaid.

"Duncan! It's the New Pitsligo Bread and Biscuit Works!"

Duncan's father owned the New Pitsligo Bread and Biscuit Works. The only bakery within fifty miles. Duncan so proud that he brought to Canada the little burgundy-bound hard-cover book with yellowed lined paper, like a ledger, recipes scratching its pages in his father's sharp handwriting:

> Brown Bread
> 1 stone Cerovine
> 1 stone flour
> 4 oz fat
> 4 oz salt
> 2 oz yeast
> 4 oz sugar in yeast
> 12 oz gluten
> 7 ½ pints water . . .

And his father's schedule:

> Mondays, Wednesdays, Fridays:
> 25 Stone bread – 5:30 a.m.
> 5 Stone brown nutmeg cakes – 6:30
> 3 Stone Vienna cakes – 8:00
> Tea Cakes – 10:00
> Plain cake – 1:00 . . .

Roslyn is leery of British baked goods as a result of Mr. Kipling's Cherry Bakewells. Duncan had raved about Mr.

Kipling's tarts, never available in Canada. Then they stumbled on The British Pantry one snowy afternoon while shopping, shortly after Duncan moved in — Duncan loves to shop for women's clothes — women will stop Roslyn in any store, in any country, to ask if Duncan has a brother, as he leads her around the shops, laden with shopping bags. "Try this one, it's D'Oraz, Kaliko, Jones New York." But lately she has the nagging suspicion he's trying to dress her like Harriet, all stripes and dress pants, and evening dresses she has no occasion to wear. In *The British Pantry* that afternoon in Calgary, Roslyn flipped through copies of *Hello!* magazine, catching up on the latest escapades of the royal princes, on Madonna's workout schedule, while the woman who runs the store measured stale wine gums on the scale and pointed out the new gravy mixes, and she and Duncan discussed the various ways Calgary is inferior.

Then Roslyn saw them — Mr. Kipling's Cherry Bakewells — and brought a package of six to the counter over Duncan's sudden protestations. "No, no, why not have some Curly Wurly Squirlies? They'll be more to your taste. Here — a tin of treacle and sponge!" How Roslyn had laughed that Duncan had talked up those cloyingly-sweet stale tarts filled with awful, hard-packed white icing, a dry maraschino cherry plopped on top, and Duncan turned crimson with a shamefaced anger he never forgave her for. Duncan continued to frequent *The British Pantry* weekly for his fix of rubbery Maynards wine gums until they left Canada, but Roslyn was no longer allowed.

"There. You've seen it. Satisfied?" Duncan says of The New Pitsligo Bread and Biscuit Works. "Goodness me, aren't you the silly Canadian goose." He claps his hands. "Aunt Midge is waiting. Let's be off."

Roslyn swings her purse strap over her shoulder.

"Roslyn! It's raining! What are you doing?" Duncan twists in his seat. "You're not going *in*." But Roslyn has already bent her body out against the rain. He reaches for her, misses, grabs the steering wheel as if he would commence driving away from the passenger's seat. "Roslyn!"

"Come on, Duncan!"

Roslyn shuts the car door, looks the wrong way, and is nearly creamed by a wood-sided milk truck, the driver honking, flinging his arms and rumbling past her nose. Duncan throws up his own arms, but not before she sees the telltale cheek-splotches that signal she's gone too far. He turns away and lights a cigarette, a rare habit, which will give her a headache. Roslyn crunches down the gravel in her high-heeled boots and pulls open the belled red door under the sign *Bakers of Quality*.

The room she steps into is high and cold. The first thing Roslyn notices is that the place doesn't have a smell. At least not a food smell. A peeling ceiling threatens to flake plaster bits into the dough a young girl is kneading. Roslyn bends to look through the glass. Smiles. "Hi!"

The woman behind the counter, in a hairnet, picks her teeth. She looks used, and like she blames Roslyn for it. Roslyn smiles wider, her I'm-a-bit-shy-but-harmless smile. "What a lovely village. I'm here from Canada, actually. Oh what are those? Egg tarts? Do you know, my husband's father owned this bakery at one time!"

The woman keeps on digging in her teeth, sawing a

yellowed fingernail up and down, removing turmeric-coloured seeds, giving little Pt!s when they cling to her lip.

Roslyn tries to imagine what the woman ate for breakfast. "The Bloxhams," she adds. "Duncan Bloxham. His father was Sonny."

The woman runs her tongue over her teeth. "Wha — Sonny Bloxham? Ye're haverin', lass. He nivver owned this bakery." The woman hefts off her chair. "Sonny Bloxham wis Robbie's lad. Father's hired help. Knocked up yin o' the Larsons. 1954. Nivver my business . . . whit are ye wantin', lass?"

Roslyn returns to the car, two egg pastries wrapped in thin brown paper. Duncan has shifted to the driver's seat, staring straight ahead.

Roslyn slides the second pastry onto the back seat when Duncan ignores her greasy gift. She pulls closed the door.

"Did you get what you wanted?" Duncan says coldly.

"Yes!" Roslyn says. "Yes, I certainly did!"

Duncan rewards this news with a cranked-up Tina Arena in the CD player. "16 Years." Has it already come to this? He takes off in a skid of gravel, the rental car whipping down grey wet streets, past rows of grey wet row houses under a grey wet sky until he spins left at the edge of the village, and there, rammed up against yet another field of cows, sits Aunt Midge's cottage. Just like the pictures. The house that Duncan lived in with his mother and Aunt Midge for fourteen months while his father found work in England.

If what Duncan says can be believed.

Roslyn bites down on her egg pastry. Lets the cold cream fill her cheeks.

Duncan's mother worked in a box factory in this village to pay rent to her own sister, came home nights with bleeding hands stuck full of splinters. Later, as a preteen in northern England, Duncan rose at five a.m. to stoke the fires so the house would begin to warm before she left for work. So wonderful a mother that Duncan saved his pennies to lavish chocolates on her.

Duncan parks in the muddy lane and out they climb. A chilly north wind whips up the field, bringing the smell of cold hay and damp. The door to the cottage swings ajar in spurts. A stiff tall woman pokes her head out, like a groundhog checking the weather, a woman with thin white hair flinging itself off a startled-looking head, cheek creases sagging below her chin. A scrape above her left eyebrow.

"Dunkie?" the woman stands bent forward on the threshold. A long grey cat, pencil-thin, wanders past behind her. Aunt Midge yanks Duncan through the doorway where he stops so abruptly that Roslyn tromps his heels. She peers over his shoulder, half expecting the ghost of his dead mother to offer a box-scraped hand, or his grandfather with the frighteningly-large neck to shamble into the parlour. Duncan has told her these details and others in fits and starts after rousing sessions of sex, after bringing her to pleasure, after she's kneaded and pummelled him to satisfaction and then scratched his feet. After which a flushed and tender Duncan, hair sticking up every which way, has been prone to making earnest confessions. Duncan brushes down his dandelion coif now, an anxious habit, sheds a few hairs, and shoves his coat at Roslyn. Should she lay it on the floor? Duncan is peering around her, back out the door, like he might make a run for it.

They are in a narrow living-dining room, painted the pink Roslyn expects in funeral homes. An enormous table sits in the small room's centre. Chairs line the walls as if the room were a dance hall with wallflower seating only. Dried flowers sprout on side tables, stuffed in sealers, coated in dust. The wallpaper a crisscrossing of wild geese being shot by jolly hunters. "Are there wild geese in Scotland?" Roslyn says.

"What are you on about?" Duncan, squeezing his ear-lobes, another anxious habit. Everywhere are doors. Roslyn counts five closed doors leading from the long narrow room.

Aunt Midge goes off into a wheeze. Is it laughter? Roslyn suspects nervosity. "Help ma Boab! Dunkie!" Aunt Midge exclaims, bent over, panting, as if she had just delivered a particularly naughty punchline. "Yer lookin' awfy grey aboot the gills." She slaps her knee, then changes her mind and slaps the scratched brown Bell piano. "Dae ye mind, Dunkie? Wull ah play a wee tune for ye?"

"Mother's piano," Duncan says tightly. "Is it going to the Bloxhams?"

"Och, dinnae worry, yer sister wull tak' it," Aunt Midge says. "She taks everythin'. But that's eechie ochie. Cam ben the hoose. . . . Cam ben the hoose."

Roslyn bends closer. *I hate you* is scraped into the maple wood.

"Ma Dunkie," Aunt Midge examines every inch of him with beady eyes that sit in pools of water. "Dunkie, Dunkie, Dunkie." Her collar appears to be sprinkled with bits of scrambled egg. She has thin patchy stubble on her chin.

Roslyn bends to pet the cat. The creature rises in the air, hissing and clawing. Aunt Midge sprints through one of the doors with astonishing dexterity. Through the opening Roslyn sees a tiny kitchen, and Aunt Midge flipping over-done cauliflower from a pot into a blue mixing bowl. Her burgundy stretch slacks elongate her long, thin bottom. She swims in a light blue twin set with dark blue flower sprigs embroidery-stitched around the neck. The flowers bleed into the buttonholes. Duncan pads over to the one easy chair in the parlour, decorated with lace doilies, and perches on it.

"Your Uncle Potter is ninety and a scuttle noo," Aunt Midge calls from the kitchen. She dumps out the boiled potatoes. "The auld geezer's still hobblin' aboot . . . he's no deid yet."

"Where is Uncle Potter?" Aunt Midge's younger brother, Aunt Midge informed Duncan on the telephone, ran away from the nursing home and has been holed up with her.

"Whaur's Uncle Potter?" Aunt Midge sing-songs from the kitchen. "Whaur's Uncle Potter?" She wheezes like Ros-lyn's parents' Robbins Myers fan. Roslyn envisions Uncle Potter crumpled in the hallway closet, knitting needles crisscrossing his throat. A stuffed Uncle Potter, lugged to the front room afternoons and pressed into the lace-doilied armchair that Duncan occupies. She looks to Duncan but he just says, "Where's the telly changer?" as if she would know, finds it, and commences flipping channels until he comes upon a cricket match.

Roslyn looks at the huge mahogany table sitting smack dab in the middle of the room, like a ping-pong table. No way of getting straight from Point A to Point B. "Could I set the table for you?"

"We dinnae use it," Aunt Midge says, sticking her head

through the doorway. Roslyn shoots Duncan a triumphant glance. To hear him, every Brit dresses and sits down for formal dinners seven days a week. But then, their San Fulgencio neighbours have shifted *that* view! It's turning out Duncan's usually wrong. Keeps a person's spirits up living with someone who's mostly wrong. Aunt Midge is hacking pieces off a well-done roast beef. "Tis Potter's favourite, so 'tis. Sunday roast, tatties and a wee dram and he's fu' as a puggie."

Aunt Midge points with a handful of silverware to the end of the room where little tin TV trays with fox-hunting pictures line the walls. Roslyn takes the cutlery.

"The plates? They're awer there."

Roslyn walks between living room and kitchen, around and around the table, setting the three TV trays. Then Aunt Midge sets them all over again because Roslyn placed the glasses incorrectly and the dessert spoons should be above the plate, handle facing *right*. Fortunately Duncan is engrossed in cricket and doesn't share Aunt Midge's chuckle.

The scrambled egg–like linings on Aunt Midge's collar sprinkle off as she trots back and forth fetching the cauliflower, Brussels sprouts, peas, two kinds of potatoes, roast beef, and Yorkshire pudding. She crowds these serving bowls on the two extra TV trays against the adjacent wall and they sit to eat. Aunt Midge eats fast and bird-like. She looks as if she doesn't get a lot of food inside her. She and Duncan keep a close eye on their roast beef and cricket. God knows where Uncle Potter's got to. Roslyn contemplates the mahogany dining room table with its thick coarse grey blanket, yellow-trimmed.

Duncan, his usual elegant manners abandoned, crams in mouthfuls of Sunday roast and squints at his food. After a bit, he rises and flicks on the light.

"Help ma Boab! Ye'll he' ma table legs a' bleached!" Aunt Midge cries, and hops up to flick it back off. The front door opens abruptly, and Duncan's sister walks in. Roslyn recognizes her from her photo on Aunt Midge's mantle.

"Aha!" the sister says as if she caught the three of them there in the gloom in a compromising act.

"If it isn't the fancy piece herself," Duncan says and wipes and wipes his mouth against his napkin. A pea rolls off his plate.

"The Beauty of this World Hath Made Me Sad," his sister sneers. She sticks her jacket on a contraption sitting by the door that Roslyn now sees is a coat tree, and pours herself tea at the kitchen counter from the teapot under the tea cozy shaped like a duck.

Aunt Midge flaps her arms as the sister sloshes toward the table. "Ah've had this table fower years an' twa; ne'er a blemish! Ah'll no' thole a tea-ring noo!"

The sister veers left, and sits behind the roast and mash.

"Well, aren't you a stoater!" She looks Roslyn up and down, holding her teacup on her knees and leaning forward past Aunt Midge. "I'm the sister."

"How do you do?" says Roslyn. Duncan's glower scrapes them both and the sister laughs. No one says a word throughout the entire pudding, which isn't pudding at all, but a dry hunk of loaf cake drizzled with brandy. The three have three scotch on the rocks each after tea, and then, satisfactorily drunk, as if on prearranged signal, everyone makes for the door and piles into the sister's car for a jaunt to a cousin who sent the sister over to bring back the Canadian.

"Colin's boy fairin'?" Aunt Midge asks from the back seat where she and Roslyn rock together as the sister catapults the car down the thoroughfare, whistling.

"Cam aff rigs at Easter and gave himsel' an overdose, the stupid galoot. They had tae pump his stomach. The eejit wis only joking."

"Any word o' Queenie?" Aunt Midge says, digging up her sleeve for a stained handkerchief.

"Mon!" the sister says. "Have ye no heard?" She rolls down her window. Rain and wind bluster in. "Ha'en an affair wi' a dobber while her man wis working' on the rigs — the hoor — and when Malcolm came back early that abscessed tooth botherin', and when the bloke Camen wis walking tae catch his bus tae the mine, Malcolm shot the bastard deid, turned gun and killed himsel'. Happened yesterday, so it did. We're 'ere."

"Och away," says Aunt Midge from the back seat, "it's guid tae get a bit o' news noo and then."

The cousin's house, like Aunt Midge's, is a maze of doors. They enter from the street to a long narrow hall. One door opens to a tiny kitchen, the next to a minuscule dining room, another to a small parlour, another to a bathroom, like a railway station. Roslyn mentions this to Duncan as they crowd into the parlour.

"Anything else you don't like?" Duncan says. The splotches have returned to his cheeks.

"Whit she on aboot?" the sister says.

"The weather," Duncan says.

"Where's Liam?" the sister asks the cousin who looks late twenties but is missing all her teeth. Her lap is loaded with a great pile of wash.

"Drunk aff 'is erse as usual," the cousin says. For all that she wanted to see the Canadian, she doesn't give Roslyn a word, though she keeps taking peeks as if Roslyn can only be stood in doses. "A nip o' whisky?" she asks Duncan and sends the sister into another room for it. "So. How's Canada? Cannae work mysel' oot o' here." She points to the laundry, and laughs gummily. Other laundry piles stash themselves about.

"Cam' hame fer his mither's funeral, Liam did," the sister says, "no' like some ah ken . . ." and she stares at Duncan. The cat, this one ginger, perched on top of a pile of flowered sheets, attacks something in its centre, digging her way to the bottom and then throwing herself out.

"Och he's a right scunner. Had a go at a coco pop. 'Awa an' bile yer heid,' he telt the polisman. Got himsel' arrested afore we left the airport," Aunt Midge tells Duncan. "Spent the night in the nick. It's a wonder he made the funeral. The big gowk's back on the rigs."

"He's no' canny wi' his money," the sister says. "Goes like thread through a needle."

"Och, he's no' a bad lad; he sends me a wee stipend now and then," Aunt Midge says, pleased.

One of the doors opens and a passel of little girls pile onto the sofa, staring at Roslyn, dresses ranging from the colour of corn husks to molasses. They sit with their feet out like pegs in a row.

"A' the wee cousins, tegither, " Aunt Midge says to the

girls. "Noo, stop yer footerin' aboot and tell me hoo yer keepin'."

"Tickety-boo," says the biggest one.

"Hunky-dory," says another.

"We wis watchin' the telly, Auntie Midge."

"Were you really?" Roslyn says because they're all staring at her.

The little girls tumble over laughing.

"Say somepin' else," the littlest orders.

"Well, we're living in Spain," Roslyn says, taking Duncan's hand. The little girls fall off the sofa in a rollicking heap, one kicks another in the head and suddenly everyone is slapping.

"Gazpacho soup, *atún* and olives," the sister says. "That's whit you'll find in Spain."

Duncan withdraws his hand. The sister gulps her scotch. "Pudding is mushed raisins wi' pine nuts. The Spanish couldnae make a bloody roast beef sandwich tae save thersel' . . . nivver mind a mutton pie. But Britain's nae guid fer the likes o' Duncan."

"Dinnae tell me yer gonnae vote for Franco?" Aunt Midge says.

"Aunt Midge, Franco's dead."

"Stop fidgeting wi' yer mither's plant!" Aunt Midge tells the biggest to cover her embarrassment.

"I wiz just sat-sitting," the girl says sulkily.

"Whit's your address?" the sister asks.

"A' widnae mind a wee holiday!" Aunt Midge says.

"Don't have it offhand," says Duncan at the same time as Roslyn says, "I've got it in my purse."

"You don't," Duncan says.

"Missus, dae ye no' ken a purse fae a handbag!" one of the little girls says. They fall all over, giggling and slapping. Wind and rain buffet the rattly windows.

"Yer a cheeky bunch o' lassies," Aunt Midge says. "Ye've got oor Canadian fair puzzled."

"What happy girls!" Roslyn says because everyone's still looking at her as if expecting a response. "If you're as good a mother as Duncan's mother was, they're very fortunate."

The room hushes. The cousin looks past Roslyn's ear. Even the little girls stop squirming. The sister laughs into the silence.

"Whit she on aboot noo?" says Aunt Midge.

"Aren't ye a strange one," says the cousin disapprovingly.

"Well, I just mean Duncan had such happiness as a child," Roslyn says.

Duncan's face is blotchy. "Aren't you something."

The cat leaves the room.

Everyone has more whisky, Roslyn included, and they drive back through hurtling rain, the sister grinding the gears, Duncan grinding his teeth, Aunt Midge muttering, "Ye wis happy?! Ye wis lucky somebody agreed ta bring ye up!"

The sister guns it out of Aunt Midge's driveway before the car doors are closed. Aunt Midge complains of an ailing stomach and goes straight to bed with a large glass of brandy.

Roslyn crawls into bed in the spare room where she and Duncan engage in polite, silent sex under a picture of the Queen. Duncan's rasps reminiscent of Aunt Midge's wheezes.

"I meant to ask you," Roslyn says the moment the act is done, Duncan still beneath her, tousled and eager. "Was your mother a Larson? No, I didn't think so. Because your father? He was just hired help at the bakery. Oh, and he got a Larson pregnant. Two years after you were born."

Duncan lies still as a plucked bird. Roslyn extricates herself from their pile of sweaty limbs and marches into the parlour, leaving him prone on the creaky bed.

The house is cold and dark. Moonlight sweeps the table, bleaching its perfect legs. Despite the cold, the parlour air is stifling. Roslyn finds it hard to breathe. She thinks of Harriet, car wheels grinding her jewellery into the mud. She grabs her coat from the wonky coat rack and steps into the blustery night just as Aunt Midge's bedroom door scrapes open and out she pops in a flowered flannel nightdress, pink fuzzy slippers, and a nightcap lifting in the wind sweeping through the open door.

"Aff fer a daunder, hen?" Aunt Midge calls, as if that's what Canadians do, go for night drives in their pyjamas. "Or waitin' fer yer morning' parritch? Here, let me get ma lozenges oot. Ma sweets. I keep 'em hidden doon the seat o' ma chair so I don get at 'em. Go oan . . . tak' twa. Keep yer teeth frae chatterin'.

They sit in the dark, Roslyn and Aunt Midge, straight-backed at the TV trays, chewing candies. Duncan soundless as death in the room adjacent.

It is that field out the parlour window, that endless empty field butting up against the house that gets to Roslyn, and all those moon-faced Aberdeen Angus cows in a semi-circle. Not even smart enough to hope.

The
Sewers
of Paris

———

Eggs make her sad. And if she fucking feels like feeling sad, she will. Stella throws herself onto her lumpy couch. At her ex-boyfriend's family reunion, they invented an egg recipe called Pan. Terry's parents are from rural Saskatchewan. Run-to-the-barn-and-kill-a-hog. Terry grew up on stewed pigs' feet. Bread pudding. Blood pudding. Rice pudding. Emerald jello studded with raisins and shredded carrots. Marshmallow and walnut coleslaw. A meat-and-potatoes boy, twelve years her junior, with a penchant for the exotic. He likes Ethiopian swordfish, sex on the edge of sloughs, fast-walking, Ekonos on Sunday afternoons, and public washrooms with those paper towels that descend on their own.

What he doesn't like is her.

Terry was *the one*. Well, didn't he last a year? Stella watches her pufferfish and her electric eel chase each other round and round the aquarium. She bought it the day that Terry left her. Fish tanks are good feng shui. How many times can one woman be dumped? She likely holds the Guinness World Record. Almost forty-four years old. For christ's sake, this is an emergency. Roslyn says, Forget the past. The past's a minefield. What does Roslyn know, married again and living it up in Spain? Well, Stella's in the mood to step on a mine and blow. She grabs the changer sticking out from under the couch pillows and flips on the television. Loosens the hook and eye on her scratchy form-fitting bra. It's brand new, blue lace, underwire. She bought it for her triumphant trip to Spain. True, the bra looked more luxurious on the shelf than with her in it; it's the stiff pop-up variety, the kind an eager librarian might wear. Since Terry took up with Charlene, Stella has taken up gorging on boysenberry sorbet. She has the time: what with her three-week un-vacation booked.

Brossie takes a flying leap, lands on Stella's midriff, and in one deft motion is kneading her chest, paws slow and sensual. Who wants to make love to Stella? A frigging cat. Her melted-down candle is stuck in a congealed puddle to the top of the TV. Below it, Dr. Phil is spilling the debris of a couple's life onto his studio floor, his ironed pants dangerously creased, his cologne-sprinkled chin jutting toward the snivelling husband; the audience, ninety per cent women, yodelling as an off-camera stagehand holds high a CLAP VIGOROUSLY sign. In the time it takes Stella to slap at a family of late-autumn fruit flies (October, Roslyn assured her, the perfect time to visit Spain), Dr. Phil has stamped all over the perpetrator while riding metaphorically high in his shiny leather saddle, the woman with the philandering husband sniffling along like she's doing an ad for nasal drip.

Outside Stella's bay window, down on the street, four neigh-bourhood Barbies and their six dogs speed-walk by: a borzoi, a whippet, a Boston terrier, a saluki with feathered ears, and an embarrassed Australian ridgeback, while the demented springer spaniel catapults across her lawn, leash flying, chas-ing a squirrel, the women dolled up in Lululemon, the dogs a ridiculous pell-mell of knitted sweaters and mismatched bows. Brossie abandons Stella to tail-switch at the win-dow. He tongues his cavity, cranks his neck to stare at her. Complains. Stella puts her foot down at walking a cat. She could pay four hundred dollars to have Brossie put under to fix his tooth, but this cat's prone to fainting spells; he's likely to put himself out for the operation at no extra cost.

Commercial. Toasted cereal and online dating. Stella examines her sprawled body, bleakly admiring all those dips and hollows that Terry will never again massage. Against up-drawn knees, she doodles a veined replica of Spain's Duende River on a paper napkin stained with peach juice: she and Terry were set to backpack there, ending up at Roslyn's, tick-ets already bought, before he and Charlene "ground gears," (the quotation marks belong to Terry; he loves his dirt-bike). Stella sketches the animal-pelt-pinned-to-a-wall-outline of Spain so hard her pencil impales the napkin, while on the flickering screen three guys in sweatpants hearten the Boston Pizza deliveryman with their warm cries. Brossie greedily swallows most of a piece of dental floss. Gags up a hair ball. Stella wrests the phlegmy string away, and *Dr. Phil*'s back on.

Stella has always seen herself as a pleasant person. Even Terry called her "nice" before he dumped her for Charlene.

But she can't stand the psychologist who swoops onto the screen across from Dr. Phil. Can't stand the way she opens her mouth wide and holds that gummy pose, as if speaking were ancient transcendental muscle exercise. Can't stand the way she coyly trails her hair around her ears. Can't stand how she tells the wife it's her *job* to let the husband know how she is feeling (Hon, I'm cranky because you're fucking Irene).

"Tell us about your course on self-esteem," Dr. Phil says, crossing and uncrossing his knife-pleated knees, the camera panning to his wife Robin, looking like she might start warbling there at the screen's edge, nodding, nodding from the audience, as if a question has been lobbed at her, as if with a neck-kinked whack she will volley the perfect answer back on stage.

Goat-grin: "My classes are in de*mand*!" the psychologist bleats. A Posh Spice mouth-purse. Aha! Stella spots lip lines! "Clients *demand* improved self-esteem, and I prod*uce*!" That hair-flip voice. I'm-just-so-friggin'-popular-and-am-I-not-attractive-in-a-frozen-forehead-kind-of-way? Eyes dart, she shifts and swings her knees; oh lord, the cameras caught her bad side. "My course will change your *life!*" Teeth wrapped round the back of her head. Wouldn't you know it, she's writing a book. She reads an earnest excerpt about poverty-stricken children playing on a pocked street in El Salvador. "Hungry for love, our little Paco . . ."

"We'll be back in a moment," Dr. Phil interrupts, "with more on our couple from Cleveland, and Kevin's marital indiscretions."

Stella rolls off the couch. Eggs it is. She fancies Pan. On their camping holiday in Saskatchewan, Terry's rum-soaked sister and his four ammonia-scented younger brothers were horsing around the Loon Lake campsite, "Taking Care of Business" pounding on the car stereo, the grandma gripping the picnic table's edge, protesting, "What Home, Stanley? Don't I live with you?" Staring around the campsite at the scattered dented rusty trucks with their gargantuan tires and drumming reverberations, wind chimes wheedling outside the trailer parked across the dirt path, while Terry's father pried Granny's fingers loose and drove her to Turtleford (down Highway 26, the brothers agreeing: Granny's gone off the rails) and dropped her at Lakeland Lodge in a town that boasts the largest turtle in North America (eight feet) named Ernie and is also home to the breeding grounds of a small vulnerable bird called Sprague's Pipit. Terry's father stopped in St. Walburg on the way back (home to the Blueberry Festival and his sister Eileen, and named for a nun canonized for her missionary work), so didn't return with the promised lettuce from Eileen's garden for Stella's lettuce-green-pea-cheddar-cheese-and-mayo salad, he and Eileen having headed for the Four Leaf Inn to play schmier and the VLTs.

Stella threw the peas out in the morning. Gleaming green pearls against the sand.

That evening Terry's sister from Moose Jaw showed off her juggling skills, faced backwards like a bride letting the bouquet fly, and flipped a piece of bread into the frying pan held by Terry. Julian, the brother in bowling shoes, not to be outdone, did the same with an egg. It somersaulted, spun, and broke in the frying pan, spreading itself over the bread. Terry, a vegetarian, (hence Stella's thoughtful lettuce-green-pea-cheddar-cheese-and-mayo contribution) pulled out the broken shell. Co-ol, everybody said. And Pan was born.

Turn on the heat.

Smear. Fry. Flip. Salt and pepper.

An egg-laced work of art.

Stella slips her Pan onto a plate swiped from a teetering wall of dishes in the sink. Brossie pads the counter top, investigating, upends the jar of bird of paradise Stella bought herself when Terry's surprise exit signalled *hasta nunca* to the myth of Spain. Its orange petal-beaks stab the pooled floor. Brossie straddles the prostrate flowers and laps up the green and stagnant water. Stella heaves the drooping beaks into the garbage. Suicide by proxy. Suicide by trash.

She plunks back onto the couch, chewing her rubbery concoction while considering all the exotic flowers of Spain, and what splendid swears they make: *Espina Santa! Hierbo en Cruz! Tomate del Infierno!*

She and Terry managed one trip—to the north of France. At the last minute his four brothers clocked time off and tagged along. The heart of Paris, it turns out, is in its sewers. No really. Sewers or the Eiffel Tower? Sewers or Moulin Rouge? They descended, all six in one hearty Canadian clump. An hour and forty-seven minute wait while the security guard had lunch. Thirty-eight degrees and humid, no public washroom in sight. They formed a queue in that sticky whack of Parisian heat along with a milling group of surly Aussies in plaid trousers and hats as loud as they were, fed up with foie gras, fed up with the bloody frogs who ignored them when they yelled questions in English. Whackers!

The sewers stank. The air alight with dank, clogged drains,

stagnant vegetable slime, the whiff of decomposing rat. Stella held her breath. Held her bladder, sucking in like a vacuum cleaner. She pictured Jean Valjean, buttocks clenched, moist back pressed against a dripping wall, Inspector Javert, rat-like whiskers, tripping by, hunting him down for the heel of a loaf of bread. While the sewer ceilings creaked and groaned under passing bus tours, the brothers exchanged ideas about Scrub Free versus Vim. That night, all six of them sweltering in one hotel room, the brothers got the swell idea to drag the bedclothes off the bed, fill the tub with icy water, dunk the sheets, and play a version of snap-the-wet-tea-towel until asses were shiny red. Eventually they all lay in a row on the worn floor, a tangle of sweaty limbs, rug-burned buttocks, pulled the cold wet sheet over them, and dripped together under stained cotton while the traffic of Paris roared by.

The doorbell chimes. Stella smacks down her plate, sprints, shedding cat hair as she goes, sweeps open the door, fist crackling like a light bulb. If Terry dares to imagine —

"Sigh," the man on the front steps says.

Stella exhales. Brossie darts. The man in the light blue silk pants and gold-metal shirt (TV Mafia?) catches Brossie's head in the door with a dull clunk.

The man's shirt is open at the neck, sprouty chest hairs, thick gold chain. Dark greased-back hair. Cream-coloured loafers. Someone's volatile boyfriend. Definitely not hers.

Brossie sways off down the hallway, listing sideways.

"Cy," the man sticks out a square-nailed hand. Sunlight bebops off his neck chain. Parked at the curb waits a baby blue convertible. "Here to test your treadmill."

Hmmm.

Stella's basement fuse box lately blows at random. Power-surging bursts, like spits of rage. It started the week Terry walked out. Her ex was a dry man. Embraced his dandruff. Left sloughed-off skin cells on the couch. Ate cereal without milk. Refused Lypsyl. He grew up during a drought. What could he do? His favourite part of Paris was the low-flush toilets, where your shit smears down the side, but not a drop of water wasted. True, Stella called for a repairman. But repairmen don't step off *The Sopranos*, do they? Repairmen wear coveralls and LA Lakers caps; they sport tape measures and dull flattened pencils. Stella's been hoping the machine is ruined so she can get insurance money, buy fuchsia leotards, a crocodile skin dress, subscriptions to *Aerobic*, *Condé Nast* and *CosmoGirl*. When Terry was in the picture, Stella sweated forty minutes daily in his boxers and her tank top on her state-of-the-art treadmill, grimly climbing hills, while Terry sat in the wingback chair cheering her on, breathing dryly through his mouth, and watching the Parliamentary Channel. Ever since he left, Stella has ostracized the machine, lain in strips of sunlight, examining her thighs for cellulite.

"Boyfriend couldn't test it for you?" Cy leans against Stella's bookshelf, butt coyly arched.

Stella considers kicking Cy's feet right out of their cream loafers. She considers zapato assault. "He's a ballet dancer. He's on tour." Stella strides through her house and down the creaky stairs. Before Cy, light-footing behind her, can turn the corner into her exercise room, she snatches the magnetized emergency button, sticks it down her pop-up bra. The machine can't run without it.

Moments later Cy is standing over the treadmill, hands lifted as if to pronounce a blessing. Stella braces herself for a Dr. Phil-evangelist voice-over. But Cy just draws himself up, takes a tomatoey breath, and steps onto the treadmill. He stabs a button. "Let's power 'er up," he says. "Stepping in this week for my friend Joey. Won a trip to Vegas. My job? Fixing fire extinguishers." The machine blinks on and SI SI SI slides across the screen. Cy cries, "Awesome! That's my name!" His bubble butt strains as he forces the tire-tread walkway into motion. He goes, it goes. He stops, it stops.

Cy pokes at every button on the machine. "Weird. That's really weird." Cy's voice bumps in and out as he struts handsomely on the spot. He taps the machine's arms. Turns the power off, fires it up. SI SI SI. "Electricity's on, but she won't go!"

"*Most* strange!" Stella says with sharp surprise, the emergency button angular and cold within her bra.

Cy slaps the panel. "Well, she's defunct!" The two of them trip upstairs.

At the front door Cy rocks on his heels and asks for a glass of water. Stella fetches. Cy drinks. His Adam's apple bobs. He only dates agent women, Cy announces, staring at Stella's breasts. His fingers brush hers as he hands back the glass. He must use Lypsyl. The glass edge is waxy, smeared.

"Agent women? Like the CIA?"

"Agean!" Cy says, voice strident with enunciation. "Filipinas are the best."

He is looking down Stella's blouse. Does the treadmill button show?

"Asian?"

"Well, ye-ah." Cy grins. His first wife was white and dumber than a post. He leans in. Garlic laced with herbs. "Don't ever marry someone thirty IQ points lower than yours." Cy smoothes his shirt by sticking out his chest. The poor woman must fall right off the charts.

Cy's foot bumps the door. Brossie pokes his head out from behind the paper rack and hisses. No offence, Cy says, but dating Agean girls's the way to go. Want an example? Cy glances at Stella's couch. Stella glances at her watch. Will Kevin from Cleveland go straight to Dr. Phil's Sex Rehab? But Cy's already launched: End of a day — Cy's moist hand slides over hers — you just wanna sit down and soak your feet? Basin of hot water? Epsom salts? Fifteen minutes or so? Well, answer him this: Will a white woman scrape dry and flaking skin off your cracked heels? Cut out your corns?

"Ewwwww!" whooshes out of Stella.

Thank you! She's proved Cy's point.

Cy asks for another glass of water. Unless she has Mountain Dew? All that sweating on the machine. Did he say? He's planning on turning Mormon. Well, because of the priesthood! What other church has the priesthood? No, Catholics don't count. Any Mormon can become a priest and still get married. Do Lutherans, Pentecostals, Seventh Day Adventists have the priesthood? Triumphant pause. In the Church of Jesus Christ of Latter Day Saints, you can climb your way *in* heaven! Stella pictures rows of Holy Step Machines. It's the one true church. No, she just has never had it explained clearly — he'll send some literature. He'll send the missionaries. No, of course *women* can't join the priesthood. Well, good deeds are their own reward. Agean women: they're joining the church in droves. Cy sighs with relief — good thing. Why? Well, they're never fat! Cy couldn't bear eternity with someone fat. Revived by a second glass of water, Cy sweats at the thought.

"Oh, What a Beautiful Morning" from the musical *Oklahoma!* jangles. Cy shouts "Yo!" into his cell. Stella seizes the moment, wrestles open the front door with a promise to read up on Joseph Smith.

Brossie lurking cross-eyed under the credenza.

§

Days pass. The silence dries her out. It snaps like pop rocks. The telephone doesn't ring; the doorbell doesn't chime. Her hair bristles with static. She imagines being canonized. Works on her conversion to permanent singledom. Flicks light switches. Shock after jolting shock. She reads up on Ezekiel's dry bones. Drinks water incessantly. Watches re-runs of *The Golden Girls*, arm hairs sprung. Makes up *Jeopardy* questions, humming its peppy soundtrack. This famous artist painted Spain's *Guernica*. Who is Pablo Picasso?! Congratulations! You have selected the right answer! This coastal city in Spain has the largest influx of *Madrileños* every summer. What is Santa Pola?! That's absolutely correct! Choose your next category!

She makes lists of adverbs that don't end in ly. Seldom. Always. Soon. Reads how-to books: How to set up a sprinkler system; How to waterproof a tent; How to build a canoe. She signs up for paintball. Brossie opts to go along. They come home grim and satisfied, splattered in orange paint and sky-blue welts. They grow long and lean. They drink green tea, which aids stomach disorders and prevents cavities. She pulls Brossie's tooth herself. They switch to the country FM station. Make lists of songs featuring kickass boots. "These Boots Are Made for Walkin'." "Whose Bed Have Your Boots Been Under?" "Jesus, Take My Boots." "Put Yourself in My Boots, Honey." "Boots of Spanish Leather." "Puss and Boots."

Maybe Terry hung onto the tickets and whisked Charlene to *Bella España* to visit Roslyn. She buys a nail gun. Redoes her hardwood floor. Late. Very. She envisions Terry as a walking cyst, blisters proliferating under the clammy Spanish sun. Brossie moves into the dark hall closet, sleeps sixteen hours a day. She buys a waterbed. Devours cartons of blueberry Häagen-Dazs out of the container, wedged in so hard it bends the spoon.

He is only an ex. It was only one year.

Fast. Already. Now.

What she really wants is a guest appearance on *Dr. Phil* with her own mob-like maenad women. She'll paint the basement crimson for passion. Hang crystals in the window. Run a humidifier until condensation creeps her walls. She'll dye her hair indigo. Let her toenails grow. She'll turn her basement television to the Vacation Channel. Extinguish the lights. And she and Brossie will glide the bowels of her house on her soundless treadmill, two subterranean creatures, drifting through dusty motes, tramping off their sorrow.

With luck, she'll start being happy, perhaps tomorrow.

Besides
Construction

====================

"Well, holy fuck." Floyd rocks on his heels. "I haven't worked on a house like this since the 1960s." He turns in a slow circle. "Christ. The walls are out of plumb. Floors screwed to death. There must be ten pounds of nails in this hardwood. What did the hooligans you hired use to cut this wall out? A bread knife?"

"Do you want to walk away?" Roslyn says to her new contractor's back.

Floyd examines the edge of missing wall. What looks like a stapled extension cord dangles from the ceiling.

"I never walk away from a job," Floyd says. "I never walk away."

"What's the worst part?" Roslyn grips her glass of Coke, her third this morning. The house is in shambles. Leaky taps. Linoleum peeling underfoot. Cupboard hinges loose. Floyd swings open a cupboard door and a dusting of plaster salts his hair. He stands back, wraps his hands behind his neck and winces.

"Does your neck hurt?" Roslyn asks.

Floyd shrugs at a hanging flap of ceiling. "Place puts me in mind of my marriage," he says. "The second. Worst part? Whole thing."

Roslyn sits on the front steps, where she listens to Floyd thumping and banging. After a time she gets into her car and drives back to her basement suite where the silence squeezes like shrink wrap.

§

"Most important thing is stable ground," Floyd says the moment Roslyn lunges through the front door the following afternoon — she has to give a shoulder heave to open it. He says it as if he's been holding the thought since she left. "Really stable. Firm. Another guy just walked in off the street and said he used to live here. That's got to be the fifth person. Whole damn neighbourhood lived here. This one said he held parties, people got drunk, ripped their clothes and skinned their elbows, tripping against the walls." The original builder had tried to make the walls look Spanish. Stucco swirls crest like Gaudí's frozen ocean waves. Well, they're nothing like walls in Spain that Roslyn's seen. Floyd works and hums.

Roslyn's second husband hummed. Duncan read in some men's magazine that humming while performing oral sex highlighted a woman's pleasure. He was furious at her daily, but night after night, there he sprawled across the bottom of their bed, nibbling, biting, earnestly picnicking, humming tunelessly.

"A goddamn wacko built this house." Floyd kneels stiffly to pick up a screw. "Three Little Pigs could of done a better job."

Floyd's blue jeans hang off his bumless backside and his grey hair is combed straight like the teeth of a comb. So unlike Harold, Roslyn's first husband, a hulking man with thick sandy hair and a broad behind. Harold was no hummer. He was a pumper and thruster. The harder you went at it, the better it must be. Harold liked sex best after two eggs, easy over, edges crispy, and strong tea. But three years ago when Harold took his broad behind to greener pastures, Roslyn found herself waking one rainy morning, not only to no husband, but to no benefits, no RRSPs. No sex. Eight months ago she walked out on Duncan, who took his pension, three-quarters of their house, and left her the bed. She house-hunted until autumn turned to winter, until she procured a new huge mortgage on this dive in Mount Pleasant. And here she is, hoping that Floyd is some kind of house-savant who can transform this dump into a work of art. Judging from the number of bottles littering her garage floor, it's more likely his miracle will involve turning water into wine. Floyd reaches to the doorframe and his T-shirt slides from the tuck of his jeans.

"Don't have a proper footing," Floyd says to the wall in his slow deep voice. "It's similar to a woman" — he pulls a pencil stub from behind his ear and draws a line down the wall — "with big boobs and small feet. She's going to tip." Floyd crouches, keeping his neck straight, and writes something on a piece of wood, then falls silent, contemplating the task before him. After a time he says, "Now that would be a bummer." Is he referring to the woman or a problem with the wall?

Roslyn stands straight-backed in the hallway. There's no place to sit, except for one turned-over paint-pocked galvanized pail that has rolled out of the closet. Since she left Duncan, since she bought this place with its forty-year mortgage, the sorry truth is, all she thinks about is sex. Lust burbles, rising, tingling, like Coca-Cola bubbles, each time she looks at Floyd's dusty backside and carefully combed cowlicked hair. Since hiring Floyd, she's taken to wearing gartered nylons with seams running down the backs and high-heeled shoes. It makes her feel 1940s kind of sexy. She's let her hair go kinky. She's started fast-walking again.

"You're getting screwed by a law that was put in place to protect women," her lawyer told her at their first appointment. "Wrong there," Roslyn said. "I'm not getting screwed at all!" She'd laughed and honked into her balled-up tissue while the lawyer gazed pointedly away. He had a box of tissues on his desk for dysfunctional women like herself who paraded through his downtown office with variations of the same story. He was a tall, thin man who waived his initial three-hundred-and-seventy-dollar-an-hour fee for that first hour, then wrenched six thousand dollars from Roslyn's dwindling bank account for her lousy settlement. The lawyer who ended Roslyn's first marriage had been a woman, a tall and sharp-faced runner. "Amazing the steam you can run off," that lawyer had said, clenching her muscled calves. "Better than anger management classes."

Floyd is nothing like Roslyn's husbands. He's like nobody Roslyn's ever known. Sixty-four years old, a short small

man with a beer belly, methodical with his level and crow-
bar, with his slow thinking out of a problem. His speech
so unlike the lawyers' jargon, or Harold's frenzied "Okay?
Okay?" after every sentence. It was Harold who suggested
Roslyn read *The Art of Small Talk*. Harold who bought her
The Joy of Sex, pocket edition. "You can take it anywhere,"
he'd said, as if she might want to reference it at the zoo, the
corner grocer's. Roslyn beelined through icy slush to the
library the week Harold left her, and signed out on her library
card *One Hundred and One Lies that Men Tell Women.*

Floyd turns, stiff-necked, like Roslyn's Aunt Gladys
when she gets a perm, hair riding like a foreign object balanced on her head, crisp and fragile as iceberg lettuce. Floyd
peers at Roslyn with grey buggy eyes. His glasses, paint-
flecked, magnify them. "Fucking neck," he says cheerfully,
as if a day hasn't passed since she asked about it. "Woke up
one morning, mmmm, nine months ago? Piercing pain —"
he stabs both forefingers behind his head, "here and here.
Set up fucking housekeeping." He turns and rummages in
the closet.

Roslyn presses her knees together. She wants to open
Floyd up, can opener–style, and pour herself inside. "What
started it?" Her body, humming on its own.

Floyd thinks awhile. "Thinking about my ex-wife."

Floyd has slept this week in Roslyn's crooked little
house on a foam mattress in a checkered sleeping bag, having come from BC to work for her. They've agreed on a price
that will dip deeply into Roslyn's savings, but Roslyn's sister
tells her she's getting a steal. Margaret found Floyd for her.
"A solid old-fashioned builder," Margaret said. "Father was

Czech, knows everything there is to know about construction. Honest as the day is long." Roslyn was desperate; with the building boom, no contractors in Calgary would even consider taking her on for months. She couldn't sleep in this place the way it was: the chaos, the eye-searing blue of the grotty bathroom, its rotted floor and grimy walls. Margaret and Loyal had hired Floyd a few years back for their BC vacation property; he built them a gargantuan house they call "the cabin."

Margaret is seven years older than Roslyn and, since they were children, has told her what to do. Margaret aired out the unused basement suite in her house edging the golf course, and told Roslyn to move in. Charity, sort of, though Roslyn insists on paying nominal rent. Where else could she stay in Calgary these days that doesn't cost the moon? Accountants living in their cars, retired couples crashing on their grandkids' floors. So Roslyn marks papers in the dim light of the basement, under the waft of Margaret's Pork Tenderloin in Figs and Olives, and Pistachio-Crusted Chicken Breasts, dutifully climbing the stairs for dinner whenever she is asked.

That first morning Roslyn showed up at the house, Floyd eyed her with his little mouse smile and said, "You know, there's room in my sleeping bag for two!" He's working out a plan to accommodate her furniture's arrival in six weeks, though first he fixed on her his level gaze and said, "No renovation can be done that fast." But even as she felt panic tighten her torso and flash black across her eyes, he smiled and said, "Hey. Don't worry your pretty little head about it. We'll just have to hustle." He'll finish off three rooms in their entirety: floors, walls, ceilings, coving, baseboards, paint. They'll stack the furniture. Her kitchen might not be installed, the bathroom might not be painted, the spare bedroom will have to wait. But Floyd will move her in.

Evenings, after her students pack their books and disappear into the night, Roslyn drives by the house on her way home. Twenty past ten. Floyd is always there in the stark kitchen light, his small form moving about the rooms. Stepping up and down the ladder. Staring at a wall.

Day eight: Roslyn rushes over to the house after her all-day classes. She charges through the door and Floyd hangs, head first, out the attic hole and says, "Afternoon!" Dust rains as he climbs down the ladder and slaps his knees. "Mess of wires up there. Insulation's blocking air circulation from the soffits. Had to lift my fucking head off the pillow with my fucking hand this morning, or I'd still be in bed."

"How many hours a day are you putting in?" Roslyn asks, staring at his Eastern European cheekbones, shadowed by two pencils tucked behind his ears.

Floyd stands a moment, rooted to the spot, fingers fluttering his belt. "Seventeen, eighteen," he says at last. "What day did you say the movers come?"

Roslyn finds it endearing how Floyd lifts his eyes without lifting his head. How he turns his neck and shoulders as if about to gyrate into breakdancing. She likes the crooked tooth at the corner of his grin. She likes Floyd's beige paint-spattered shoes, his methodical measuring, his thoughtful gazing at a problem until the answer comes. "We'll make this pretty for you," he'll say. "We've got this under control," or, "If your heart is set on it, that's what we'll do." Roslyn, who has nothing under control, whose heart ricochets wildly, is used to husbands who do what they want to do, and then blame her. She feels so grateful for Floyd's plural pronoun, she longs to massage his neck.

Instead, she offers him her baking.

"Had a second cousin hit by lightning once," Floyd says, looking into the Tupperware container of homemade White-Chocolate Chocolate Cookies with Macadamia Nuts that she baked at the suite. "Thanks. Don't eat till supper."

"You don't eat? Nothing?" Roslyn says. "Nothing at all?"

Floyd turns and moves down the hall like he's carrying a sheet of glass, though all he has in his hand is a paper cup of Tim Hortons coffee. He clasps his hand behind his neck, tips his head and drinks. A feminine-looking bracelet, gold and silver, gleams against his wrist hairs. Roslyn scurries into the back yard under the pretext of hunting for something in the garden shed, waves of yearning pleasure striking like lightning, through her entire body.

She is paying rent and a mortgage, plus storage for the pieces of furniture she wrestled from Duncan. She wants to pay forever to keep this weathered man on the premises. This man who looks at her house and sees *her*. "What's the worst floor you've ever done?" she asks to keep him talking.

On the evenings she doesn't climb the stairs to eat at Margaret's, Roslyn prepares the same meal. A bit of oil in the pan. Fry chopped onions. Cut up a carrot and a bit of spinach. Throw in a hunk of salmon or a pork chop. Fry. She is forever hungry. She chews, overcome with such wrenching panic she has to hold her fork in midair until it passes. She's gained perspective these long months looking out Margaret's basement window while she chews. A spruce tree, a squirrel, the occasional cat, poplar fluff. When Margaret descends the stairs after dinner, knocks on the suite door and calls Roslyn up to watch *Sex and the City* or to look at her garden plants, "Sorry! I'm working! Can't chat now!" Roslyn hollers. Margaret isn't one for displays of grief. Get over it. Get a handle on it. Buck up. Move on. Nor for displays of desire. An insatiable Margaret? No picture emerges.

"Worst floor? Guess that would be the one the termites got into in Arizona." Floyd nods at the wall before him, "Got to do 'er right." He sticks more shims under the battens. A half-full beer can, its top dented, sits against the wall. "The lightning strike? That was my cousin Dagmar—Doukhobor, used to take her clothes off—struck by lightning on the old ringer phone." Floyd drains his coffee and takes a swig of beer. "She was rubbering on the party line. Sent her sailing across the kitchen with a blackened ear."

Roslyn, peering at the creases beneath Floyd's ear, leans against a wall and snags her mohair sweater. He'd showed her how far the walls leaned out of plumb, asked her if he should straighten them, and when Roslyn said no, he straightened them anyway. She shifts her weight. Floyd eyes her stockinged legs. "Can't stand crooked lines."

Are her seams not straight?

"Do that again."

Oh god, do what?

"Move on the spot. You hear that? A fucking squeak. If I didn't straighten the walls, doors would be closing and opening by themselves. You can't have that. You can't do a job halfway."

Roslyn thinks of Harold, the procrastinator: New plates? Whatever for? A few chips never hurt anyone! Paint the living room? A professional painter did it ten years ago! Replace the cupboards? Maple was built to last. He'll put in a screw to hold the door shut. Harold, the duct-tape king.

Harold left Roslyn on a Saturday morning during a November rainstorm. Roslyn left Duncan in the middle of the night during an August heat wave, the day they went to the garden centre to find some linden trees to hide the view of their neighbour's yard. The neighbour's fat scruffy cat would skulk evenings down an imaginary line between the two houses and disappear into the trees that marked the drop-off to a neighbour's yard below. When they'd moved back from Spain — at Roslyn's insistence — Duncan refused to live in Calgary, so they bought in a BC town on the side of a mountain, where everyone lived at an angle, looking down on someone else. The neighbour's teenage sons parked their cars on the lawn instead of on their driveway, so when Roslyn sat dutifully in the gazebo tent Duncan had shipped from England, she looked out on a rusted 1994 Pontiac and a dinged-up Chevy II.

"How about linden trees? Shall we go have a look?" Roslyn had asked over her yogurt and blueberries that morning. Duncan was turned away from her, frying himself back bacon — not that streaky bacon full of fat that Canadians like — three eggs, hash browns, two stewed tomatoes, button mushrooms, pork and beans, three pieces of toast.

Duncan flicked off the burner and slammed the frying

pan with a hiss into the sink. Bits of mushroom and butter flew. "You want to go? Let's go! No, no. You've eaten. I don't need to eat. Why eat now when you want your goddamn trees?"

At the garden centre, Duncan sped up and marched so far ahead down the curving path that at most Roslyn caught a glimpse of a disappearing arm or leg.

"What would you think of Japanese maple?" Roslyn called. Duncan swung off, detouring around a fountain. "Japanese maple would be a start toward hiding the beached canoe and that pile of wood and boards beside the cars, don't you think? Duncan?"

Duncan ground down the path. The previous day she'd told him she wanted the house they'd bought on their return to Canada switched to just her name. "Duncan! It's Theo's inheritance! I had to sell my house to buy the house in Spain. I never got any part of the one you left in England." Duncan had a pension and lived on his credit card. His philosophy was, Want to get somewhere in life? Look like you have money.

"Get whatever trees you want." Cold voice. "It'll be your house in three days. Nothing to do with me. You're paying!"

Back home, Roslyn wrestled three linden trees and two Japanese maples from the truck while Duncan smoked inside the garage.

That night he stood in the bedroom doorway. "We'll have to switch accounts around. You'll be paying all the bills from now on! Well, it's not my house, is it?"

"Duncan! Your house in England goes to your son. Mine goes to Theo. We share bills and expenses."

Duncan's face twitched.

"Duncan! I pay and you live here for free?"

"I hope your goddamn computer blows up!" Duncan swung into the room and out again, elbow pressed against the doorframe. "You know what's going to happen in three days? You haven't any idea, do you? You'll find out. Yeah, you'll find out, all right."

The scruffy cat watched with glittery eyes as Roslyn crept back and forth, heaving boxes into the car; Duncan, snoring, passed out on their bed, having finished off a case of English lager. But when, at two a.m., she maneuvered the car backwards up their hilled and L-shaped driveway, the screen door sprang open as if Duncan had been crouched behind it, waiting. Roslyn, spraying gravel, whizzed the car onto the street, Duncan chasing her in bare feet and boxers, mouth open in an anguished, "Ro-o-zz-lyn!" The neighbours' lights clicking on as Roslyn shot past.

"Would you care to read my novel?"

Roslyn jumps. Floyd is stuffing insulation into the two long rectangular holes in the living room wall — holes that served as built-in knick-knack shelves — forearms scratched red. He drapes the insulation in plastic.

"Six hundred pages so far."

"You've written a *novel*?" Roslyn says.

"Written 'er by hand. Don't know why I bother with vapour barrier. Rest of the house doesn't have it. Give it twenty, thirty years and this house will deteriorate because the builder didn't have a plan. It concerns my ex. My second ex. The first wife was a dream." He looks around the dusty living room scattered with tools. "Where did I lay my screw gun? The title? *Father in Heaven, Daughter from Hell.* Minister's daughter. I made her sign a prenup." Floyd climbs the stepladder, dust streaking his nose like a swab of makeup. "One morning she turned over in bed and said, 'You know that piece of paper you made me sign? It isn't worth shit!' Got home one night not long after. Place was cleaned out. Kit and caboodle. Computer. Camera. Tools. She even took my heads."

"Your what?"

"My trophies. She fetched fifteen hundred dollars for the antelope. Four thousand for the elk. No point reporting it. She was banging the town cop." Floyd climbs down, screw gun in hand, and disappears out back. Roslyn hears the truck door slam. He returns with photos — four deer heads perched on the wall in a semi-circle around a corner fireplace, as if at coffee, one miffed mule deer to the side, and beside him, a flamboyant-looking mountain goat. On the second photo, below the heads, stands a man with Floyd's body and a goat head.

"It's a reverse Pan!" Roslyn says. "Human body, goat head."

"Judge made her give back my stuff. Every tool returned with a missing piece. Even my computer. Couldn't use a goddamn thing." Floyd walks over and takes back the photo. "I was goofing around. Don't know why I kept it." He sticks it in his back pocket and finishes gluing the drywall sheets against the battens. "I'll be working 'til I'm ninety. She took me for everything." He tacks drywall on, then screws it. "Seven personalities, that woman had. Glue 'er and screw 'er." He stands back to contemplate his work. "One of those personalities? Worth all the others. Seventh one. Great at blow jobs."

Roslyn walks into her future study and sits down on a metal crate. She pictures Floyd kneeling. Writhing like an upright snake. She drives down the hill to The Blue Moo and eats and eats. Pear purée. Walnut bread pudding.

"How are things going?" Margaret says into Roslyn's ear one sunlit morning. Roslyn is at her desk in the basement suite, imagining scenes from Floyd's novel. Margaret has taken to springing phone calls on Roslyn from upstairs when Roslyn doesn't answer her door. Margaret's words are clipped and bright. Roslyn can hear banging and clinking over the wires. Margaret never sits down to talk on the phone. She rinses plates, bakes seven-grain bread, pulls weeds in her garden, phone pressed against her shoulder. It would be a waste to *sit* and talk. Roslyn adjusts the receiver. She doesn't have to leave for her workshops until noon. Springtime in Alberta. She watched a talk show a few weeks back that featured a woman who could orgasm on demand. On light-rail transit. On a 747. Waiting on a bus-shelter bench. She'd shift and wiggle and voilà! Her host asked her, "How about a demonstration?" Spring sails in the open window: wild winds and migraines, melting ice and the earthy smell of sloughs. Roslyn leans forward on her chair to push open the inner door to her basement suite. Crosses her legs tightly. Twitches.

"You know, we were thinking," Margaret says. The blender gives a short wheeze. "Loyal says he almost thinks you shouldn't have Floyd knock out the second wall."

"He already did. He did it. Two weeks ago."

"Roslyn! You didn't say! You need to keep us up to date. How else can we help you through? What shape is the house in by now? The wall's gone? Which wall? The kitchen-living room? A shame you paid and for nothing."

"How is it nothing?"

"Well, Theo could have done it."

"Theo lives in Kamloops, Margaret. He works. He's not available." Why mention that he hardly calls. That when he takes the receiver he's polite and cool, mostly silent, while Roslyn talks. She pictures him, glancing at his wristwatch, reading his emails.

"Just like Harold." Margaret clucks. "Theo's young and strong. We think he could help out on weekends. He doesn't work weekends, does he?" Roslyn feels an anxious roil in her bowels. Margaret's sons are realtors; she doesn't approve of Theo's burger-flipping and waitering, culminating in trips to Costa Rica and Nepal. "Have you thought more about taking out the supporting wall? *That* one needs to go. Loyal and I both think it would look so much better, broaden your living space."

Roslyn sighs, unsqueezes her knees, props open the screen door to the street, and steps outside, phone still pressed against her ear. Everything out over Elbow Drive is in motion. Cars and wind and flags and joggers. A hare hops by on the sidewalk, wackily out of place.

Floyd is out of place in the city. He hates the traffic. One morning he drove the length of Crowchild Trail to pick up inside doors, stepped into her kitchen an hour and fifty minutes later, breathing hard.

"Fucking traffic." His face had a pasty hue. "I'll be all right. I'll be all right in half an hour." He disappeared into the garage. Roslyn pictured him in the old wrecked wing-back chair, slugging three beer, gazing balefully out on the back alley with a bebopping heart. His blood pressure was astronomical. 186/160 last time he checked. "I don't do pills," he said when Roslyn suggested he see a doctor.

A little grey cat pads down the side steps to the suite. Every time Roslyn looks out that same cat is walking down her steps, waiting at her door. She never sees it leave. It just keeps grimly returning.

"Are you?" Margaret says into the receiver.

"Am I what?"

"Are you going to get Theo to paint?"

"No, Margaret, I'm not." Roslyn thinks of the gold and silver bracelet on Floyd's wrist. Such a delicate piece of jewellery for a man. She wants to drive over and pour her heart out to Floyd, invent a life: tell him she was once a chambermaid, travelled to Europe backpack-style, did an acting stint with a local theatre company, can walk on stilts. She says, "Margaret, I have to go," and slaps together a three-inch sandwich: salami, turkey slices, asiago cheese, avocado, radishes, cherry tomatoes cut in half. The more she eats, the less she weighs.

When Roslyn gets to her house one drizzly afternoon the following week, the air compressor is rattling at an ear-splitting shiver. She stands a moment in the porch. Whack! Whack! The power nailer. The compressor goes off and

"Thank the Lord for the Night Time" sails into the silence. Floyd's ghetto blaster sits on a patio chair outside the open garage door, so stuck-on with paint and sawdust it's hardly recognizable. Week three of renos. The day has grown hot. Brassy heat. The heat of spring before the rain returns. Last night Margaret and Loyal took in Theatre Calgary on their season's tickets. *Alice in Wonderland*. Roslyn, home alone, sat on the bench outside her basement-suite door and watched the peacock-coloured evening. The light was restless. Brooding. Its colours a violent spill. With no warning, she was swamped with panicked grief. It hit her sideways. She had to stand, legs planted on the sidewalk until it passed. She couldn't even separate what she was grieving. It hit like a slagging swamp. The Theo part she understands, deserves. But why does she sweat, chest ripping, at the thought of her husbands? Harold, turning his bulk to her with vulnerability. Irritating Harold, transformed in darkness as his hands reached for her thighs. Or Duncan. "Touch me like you love me," he whispered one night shortly before she left. Why does she wear the space her husbands left like a too-large overcoat? She wants to run up her rickety steps and spill her regrets, her yearnings, her shameful urges to Floyd, this guy with a gimpy neck and great hands who is sifting beauty through her house like clouds rolling across a summer sky.

Roslyn steps inside. The bathroom has one coat of Spanish Tile red. The new brushed pewter taps are installed. Roslyn walks down the hall. The ceilings and baseboards painted cream at Floyd's suggestion. The coving glistens in her bedroom. Floyd has widened the closet doors. Widened the doorways to living room and study. Has half the window casings nailed. Whack! Whack! A dazed bird trembles on a branch of her lilac tree. Serene green outside her window, rich dark warmth inside. The living room walls soft Café Crème. The kitchen's subfloor is down, as is three-quarters of the hardwood. Roslyn watches Floyd slotting pieces, the hammer tapping one against the other before the nailer does its job.

Floyd nailed his finger yesterday. She heard his yelp above the racket. She stands now, watching this small stranger, flat ass in the air, kneeling low over his power nailer. Creating a space for her. Transforming it before her eyes as Pan, in his grief at the loss of Syrinx, metamorphosed her into a reed, and the reed into an instrument of haunting music. Roslyn tap-taps diagonally across the floor so Floyd will know that she's here.

He looks up, winces, smiles. "We'll have her ready. She'll be ready for the movers. What—eight days left? A week from Sunday?" Gentle lines around his eyes. Sunlight glinting on his wrist hairs. Her mind works him into a frenzy of yelping cries and wanting fingers.

And she knows what she must do. She'll leave him to work his transformations. She'll go to Margaret's basement suite and return only when the place is ready: the day the movers arrive. She trusts Floyd. As if he reads her mind, he looks up and winks. "I have talents," he says, sitting back on his haunches, "besides construction."

§

They stand in the back yard, amidst Roslyn's too-high grasses on a sunlit day three days after the movers wrestled her belongings into the house. Floyd had to take the front door off and cut the frame to get the new fridge in. He's stuck the frame back and re-hung the door, but she'll order a wider one, seeing as the hole is cut out now. Floyd moves about the yard, building shelves for her office closet to house her books and papers.

Roslyn bends to look at a shelf's intricate edging. "How do you do that?"

"Router." Floyd holds up an object. Swipes at a wasp hovering about his ear. "You can get over a hundred bits for this baby. This one? A roman ogee. I dadoed the sides of the bookshelf walls too. See? That way each piece fits right into the other. Makes the shelf stronger."

In her tiny back yard with its poured concrete, its waving grasses and scattered lumber from the knocked-down deck, Roslyn watches Floyd dado the remaining shelves. She waded out here from between her piled furniture and sea of boxes, moving from bedroom to office to living room to kitchen and out the back door, a glass of Coke in hand.

Here in spring sunlight, a breeze stirs, lifting Floyd's hair. "My father learned his trade in the old country," he says. "Surrounded by builders. My grandfather, uncles too." Floyd rubs a hand over a shelf. "Back then they made everything with homemade tools. Even dado joints were hewn out with a hand saw and chisel."

"Was he patient, your father?"

Floyd lays the shelf aside, picks up his drink, and comes to join her. The little grey cat under her chaise longue scampers away.

"My father? My father was patient. He never said I did anything wrong. He used to let me work at things. Even if I built something wrong he let me finish." Floyd looks into his bottle, cups his neck, and drinks. "And then I had to rip the thing apart and do it right." He waves her thought away. "He wasn't angry. He didn't care about the waste of materials. You rip 'er apart and do it right. That's what I learned." The wind licks at Floyd's arm hairs. "My father was a hard man. He would never compliment you. And the reason was, 'If I say it's good, you won't do better next time.'"

The wind rushes, communing in the trees.

"Do you believe that?" Roslyn asks.

Floyd looks up at a passing jet. "I could never please him and here I am. Yeah."

"You're an artist," Roslyn says.

"My father used to build houses on a cigarette box. He'd sketch each out in pencil." Floyd's shoe draws patterns on the grass as he speaks. "He used to take a cigarette package to the town office, and say, 'This is the house I'm going to build.' They'd say, 'We need plans.' And my father would say, 'You've seen the houses I build. It's going to look like this.' Never drew a blueprint in his life." Floyd drinks. "I'm no artist. Can't even draw. But I can follow a plan without a blueprint." He touches his forehead. "Give me a picture. I'll create it."

Roslyn looks through the open doorway to her boxes heaped from floor to ceiling. The doors lying on the back steps. The scattered tools. The sawhorse in the centre of her kitchen. Covings, casings, intricate lines, luxurious dark floors, her own study with her own library.

"How's your neck?"

"It hurts."

"Do you think about them? The houses? Do you think about a house once it's done?"

"I could detail almost every house I've ever done. Every mistake. How I fixed her. Every challenge. How I thought her through. The railings. How I finished the basement." He runs his finger down the seam of his dusty jeans. "Oh, you don't think about them every day. But there are instances—"

"How do you deal with it?" she blurts, "the grief? Your exes?"

Floyd looks away. The wind keens, high and reedy. "I leave it inside me," he says. "In its own place."

He gets up and begins to sand. Roslyn stays on her garden chair in her bare feet and listens to the swish-swish of the rasp. In her imagination she gives him everything. And then it comes, the swift strange swoop of grief.

"Your place was a dump, Roslyn," Floyd says over the wind. "But you got nothing on this next house I'm doing. Deteriorated wood foundation. Windows all have to be changed. Roof tiles replaced."

She is startled. She has forgotten he has other jobs.

"The woman? Got a behind like a luxury cruise. I'd nail 'er in a New York minute."

Roslyn flushes hot. What was she thinking?

"Roslyn," Floyd says. "It gets easier. Did I tell you deer come to my deck?"

And she sees him, years hence, bent over his mitre saw in some other woman's back yard, sawdust flying, a round circle etching the back pocket of his flat ass like a tin of camphor salve. A healing balm. Pausing, cradling his neck, lifting his head to drink. She takes these pictures, what she could give him, what he gives her.

The lovely lap of grief.

"How much would a deck cost, Floyd?"

His back is to her. "Depends on the wood."

"If I save the money by next year, will you build it for me?"

She's paid Margaret her last rent cheque. Roslyn flexes her bare tight legs.

"Roslyn." The rasp swish-swishes against the wood. "You draw me a picture. I'll come."

In Which Jesus Hitchhikes the N332 and the Girl Tries Not to Vanish

═════

There goes Jesus, riding the back of a truck that's burning rubber down the N332. Hitchhiking on a lorry load of canned tuna, eyes pinned to the passing landscape, crown of thorns jauntily askew. The girl watches him hurtle by, his legs a blur above his strappy sandals. Lucky Jesus. What he will see with his terrible black eyes in the northwest cities he is speeding toward! The girl lists those cities in her head: Salamanca, Segovia, Palencia, Burgos, Avila. Catholic strongholds. Thousands of mud-baked fields with mud-baked castles rising from mud-baked hills between real *España* and this southeastern strip of Mediterranean Spain, where the Costa Blanca inhabitants have razed palm trees to make way for the foreigners and their high and narrow egg yolk–yellow villas. The Costa Blanca, where British accents reign the streets, and sand rains from the sky. Where British pubs sell bingo cards and crack cocaine and karaoke, British stores sell crème fraîche and double cream, where travelling hair-dressers with scissor-sized suitcases visit the high crammed houses, climbing stairs to men who cop a feel in return for a trim and a shave. No one who lives in an egg-yolk villa trusts the Spanish. Well, they're *different*, aren't they then?

The girl imagines Jesus has had it with beach holidays. He is taking his long, flowing crop of sandy hair out of the levanter wind, and scramming.

The girl in her beach dress, seated beside her husband under their cream-and-pistachio-striped umbrella, has just turned twenty-four. Everyone, even her husband, calls her "the girl." It's how she has come to think of herself. *Another* Canadian! the neighbours said to her husband when he introduced her round. No one asks her name. Most of the foreigners here appear closer to fifty than twenty-five. Of course she's "the girl"! Many have tipped into their senior years — granny years, the girl's husband says, as if men don't grow old, don't drink with deeper desperation, don't holler at three in the morning and dance like parrots to prove — well — something. The girl brushes back her shiny brown hair, crosses her fine ankles. She's different. Maybe dangerous. Everyone waiting for her to make some ghastly un-Brit gaffe. Her husband front-and-centre in the audience. She feels his disapproving stare when he pulls on his Easter-egg designer shirts, dressing for dinner.

The girl stares after Jesus, who has disappeared down the N332 in a whoosh of flying curls, smelling of black grass in the ditches. Soon the lorry will turn onto the highway to Madrid. The Spanish newspapers still write the occasional article alluding back to the Madrid bombings. The girl was barely twenty, still living at home in Vancouver, Canada, but she knows her history. Spanish elections were held shortly after. In an astonishing overthrow, the Socialists defeated the ruling *Partido Popular*. The girl defeated her mother, but now she can't go home. Her mother said, You made your bed. You lie in it. That bed is here on the Costa Blanca.

The girl's mother gouged all their furniture: the Ethan Allen cherry walnut table, defaced by zigzag slashes. Her grandmother's bureau in the hall, chunks splintered off. The antique lingerie dresser in the back bedroom, four drawers smashed. The coffee table harbours angry Xs. The leather couches, scribbled with black felt pen. The ladder-backed chairs in the salon, crosspieces cracked and snapped . . . *Covet these possessions, why don't you, while you wait for me to die!* The girl will remain here on the used-to-be-Spanish coast with the other foreigners who loll the beaches, skin hue and texture running from lobster to leather. Dark taste of citrus in their drinks. Oranges hang like copper moons in narrow Moorish streets.

The girl picks up the *Sunday Times* sticking out from her beach bag. The back of her ankles sting. Yesterday in the Mercadona, while buying tilapia and mangoes, an enthusiastic fifty-year-old man with bad teeth ran over her heels with his mother's wheelchair. The girl turns a rattly page, bracing against the wind. The paper flaps; its news cannot be contained. The girl pays six euros each weekend for the *Sunday Times*. She scans an article on anti-social behavior. Old people in Bristol are afraid to leave their homes. Roaming gangs of teenagers in hoodies whing potatoes out of nowhere, clipping the old on the ear. Girls on London streets outside rain-glistening pubs are dropping their knickers at an alarming rate. Kids in Holme on the Wolds run amok through the town's one library, terrorizing readers.

The girl sticks in her earbuds, scrolls through her iPod and settles on Band of Horses. She squints against the sunlight glaring off the sea. Her toe catches her St. Christopher medal, half buried in the sand. St. Christopher, the patron saint of travel, the medal her Catholic father gave her when she was barely ten. Though she has given up on her father's religion, and though St. Christopher has since been purged from saint-lists, the girl still prays to him. She picks up the medal, holds it in her open palm.

This morning, her neighbour's mutt, who suffers from borderline personality disorder, stalked a cat and killed it. The owners leave the dog on the roof in blasting forty degree heat, no water. Walking from table to bathroom to garden, the girl hears his sharp cries. When the neighbours, a man on the lam from the police, his girlfriend who parades her designer bathing suits in glinty sandals, and their endless visiting relatives pile home at day's end, drunk from the beach, drunk from the pub, drunk from shopping in white-domed Alicante, they haul their sandy towels, their loot and their stumbling selves through the doorway, then spill back out onto the porch, new drinks in hand. Eventually someone remembers to let the dog down. A spinning flash of fur. He bites. They whack. He bites. They wallop. He bites, goes flying. Gets shut up on the roof. No water.

This morning the girl watched a fine-boned Spanish woman in a full-skirted flowered dress (where did she come from?) and stiletto heels carry a large bouquet of calla lilies upside down to the dumpster and fling them in.

This morning the girl burned her index finger on the public pay phone. Eleven in the morning. Already thirty-nine degrees.

The girl doesn't know a single Spanish person. She is getting to know the English: her neighbours don't like their hair washed at the hairdressers because they can't bear touch. They don't like salads with their meals. Salad is rabbit food. What they hanker after is battered fish and chips and mushy peas.

The girl's husband, thirty-five years her senior, cracks his sixth beer. He too is reading the *Sunday Times*. But only the pages that say what he wants to hear. The girl tries to remember how this man came to be her husband. How she became the third wife of a man only months after he divorced his second. She makes a disorganized list. It had to do with expensive dinners, a second-hand clothing store in Salmon Arm, with rutting elk, Canadian immigration, telephone calls across crackling wires, tears (his), frightening dreams of attacking ostriches (hers), a domineering ex-wife in England (his first), a suet recipe (bird pudding) using Crisco instead of lard. She adds the man's talk of foreign places, the way he licked her. How when he stood naked he reminded her of the pet turtle she had as a child, of whom she was very fond. She thinks of his first wife who threw scissors. His second, who ran off with all of his possessions in the middle of the night. She thinks how, if she hadn't been hitchhiking through BC, she never would have met him. She thinks how kind he was to her. How he picked her up on the highway. Bought her dinner. Paid for her hotel room. Listened to her hard-luck story. Shared his own.

A teenager with a belly-button ring trots up in a white string bikini. "Don't you look like your mother," says a large woman sprawled near them on the sand, bathing suit top off, huge breasts flopping. "Don't she, Tom?"

"Dead and grey?" Bikini girl drops to her knees in the sand. "I look like a heap of ashes?" She takes a slug from her father's beer. Grabs one from the cooler.

Teenagers today are surly.

Bikini girl's belly button glints. She draws angry calligraphy in the sand and says to the topless woman, "You can snog me dad, but each time, me mum, she's watching from that paisley sack up on the mantel."

Bikini girl sashays away.

"She don't like me, Tom, she never liked me," the woman says, all indignant varicose veins and wobbly underarms. The man breathes an irritated, "Ahhhhhh," and turns on his back like a large roasting bird.

"Donna! You're blocking the sun," the girl's husband says. When on rare occasion he uses her name, he keeps it in its own sentence. *Donna!* Then he chuckles and says, Perfect name for a prima donna! The joke is old. The girl's mother is the prima donna. When news came from the clinic that biopsy samples had been mixed up, that her mother's breast was right as rain, her mother hung up the phone and dyed her hair blood-orange. Joined a breast cancer survivor group. They held potlucks every second Tuesday and discussed New

Age novels with overwrought endings while the girl's father perched on splintered edges of the furniture—a bewildered history professor with a trickle of Spanish blood—snagging his shirts, clinging to his trousers a thin grey felt tip outline from the couch pillows, reciting snippets of Spanish history: *Have I mentioned what the mother of the Nasrid king said as the Moors fled the Alhambra in 1269 before the Christian onslaught? You weep like a woman for a kingdom you could not defend like a man.*

The wobbly woman staggers up and plunges into the sea. The girl doesn't care for the sea and she doesn't care for memories. She leaves this gritty sand, harsh salt, loud foreign men who pee in people's flowerpots on their way home from the pub. She catches up to Jesus. They pass walls of convents holding brown-baked faith. They walk hand in hand past the marble slabs of Novelda. Jesus no longer smells of weeds; his scent has shifted to new-cut grass of which there is none in the Costa Blanca, just tiles and coloured pebbles to cover the bleak cracked ground. They begin to climb a hill. "Have you ever been to Vancouver?" the girl asks Jesus.

The girl and Jesus pass a Moorish church built all of pebbles. Jesus suggests a snack. They eat chorizo and a slice each of potato pie. They stop in a museum to scan pages charcoaled in Arabic script. Stone walkways, century-worn. Dripping walls and gardens. Iron benches in the plazas where iron ladies read iron books. And bulls. So many planted-iron bulls on hills. Above, Spain's thin blue sky. The girl and Jesus come upon an iron woman with four breasts lying on her back, ankle crossed over a knee, gazing sideways at a choco-churro stand.

The levanter lifts the towel's edge. Lifts the girl's fine hair. *Take the case of Gaspar de Guzman, he kissed the prince's chamber pot,* the girl's father might be saying. *His downfall was salt tax. Felipe II didn't change his clothes for years.*

The girl rifles in her beach bag, dabs sunscreen on her nose, followed by MAC shine blotter. She has no friends. In Salmon Arm, in the weeks her husband organized their trip to Spain, she was friends with Sunday. The girl pulls out her BlackBerry and texts *Hola chica,* but Sunday knows no Spanish, and if she did, still would not answer. The girl folds her section of the *Sunday Times,* drops her St. Christopher medal in the beach bag, and closes her eyes. Sunday's face clinked with metal studs and rings. She wore Indian cotton dresses that she dyed herself, so her skin took on hues of forget-me-not and melon. The girl asked Sunday to be her bridesmaid while they drove to the movie theatre. Sunday said only if she could carry Canadian thistles, the ones with the spiked purple flowers. She said Canadian thistle would present a nice tonal contrast to the ice-blue bridesmaid dress. The girl wasn't planning on an ice-blue bridesmaid dress. Thistles are a good hardy plant, Sunday said, resistant to bad weather, and they have quite dense flower heads. It was pouring rain. The car began to hydroplane. The girl slammed on the brakes and they side-swiped three cars. The girl and the man who is now her husband married fast on a Monday morning halfway up the mountain, so the husband could hightail them to Spain. He'd spent the middle part of his short second marriage in Spain with a Canadian who didn't understand his needs. Canadians aren't valued abroad, her husband said. You're not part of the European Union. No one knows you exist. However, you'll be fine because you're with me. Sunday worked the early shift at the Java Jive. They held the wedding without her.

If the girl and this man who is her husband didn't leave the Costa Blanca coast now and then to travel Spain, the girl would peel apart and blow away.

"Do you have the time?" the girl asks her husband. Her watch says ten past twelve. She cannot believe it hasn't filled with grit and slowed.

The husband dislikes if the girl points out the time. Since their arrival in Spain, he takes particular exception if she states a fact. Last week, when the girl corrected him on some detail about the Iraq war concerning British soldiers set on fire, her husband threw a bag of fresh fish on the ground — it gave a splotchy smack — slammed down the trunk lid, and said, "I don't know why people worship Jesus when they could worship you."

The husband got into the car and took off in a skid of gravel. The girl picked up the bag and stood in the middle of the road. The husband had the only keys to their house, so after a while the girl climbed to their high, thin porch, where she stared at the long strip of Mediterranean across the lumpy hills, then counted the tall thin bird of paradise blossoms in pots at her feet. Each plant had seven. Jesus materialized in a small courtyard, clapping a flamenco beat, hair and sweat flying, while a *gitano* bawled a *canto jondo*, the cry of the oppressed. Jesus began to dance, heels pounding the earth. The girl felt an earthquake rumble, a volcanic eruption. The girl's mother coped with her hard nut of anger by piling stacks of hoarded cardboard in unexpected places.

What was the girl to do?

The husband was gone only nineteen minutes. He'd tossed his wallet on the telly when he carried the first bags of groceries in, and so took off without it. How could he drink? He walked in whistling, pretending he'd felt like coming home.

The girl traces the cover of her book, Millar's *The Rules of Partial Existence*. Her husband has flipped it shut, ignoring her bookmark in the sand, but it doesn't matter; the girl had already lost her place. She thinks of King Felipe II, who lived in El Escorial, and spent his last days in his meagre bedroom overlooking a chapel, obsessively collecting priceless books. By his death, he had gathered 14,000. The girl thinks how these same books sit in the Royal Library of El Escorial today, all shelved backwards, spines facing in, the gold-leaf edges facing out. So the pages can breathe, her father told her. Breathing, her father said, enhances preservation.

A breath of wind. Here on the Spanish beach, the wind has nothing to do but blow itself around. The foreigners have nothing to do but drink. The girl has nothing to do but dig her toes into the pebbly sand. The Spanish have nothing to do but hide. "Where are the Spanish?" the girl asked the first months she was here. Her neighbours felt this to be an unreasonable question. "Why don't you go back to America?" they said. The Spanish, she thinks, have fled.

"You want to drive two hours to gawk at a clammy cave?" her neighbours say if the girl cajoles the husband into travelling up-country for the day.

"They're the Caves of Canelobre!" the girl says. "Franco hid there."

Nobody gives a toss where Franco hid. The girl and her husband sometimes drive to Guadalest. To the town built into natural stone. To the castle with hundreds and hundreds of stairs that lead nowhere, that end at nothing.

On their last up-country jaunt, the girl said, "What do people in England do for their birthdays?" to make conversation once they were on the carriageway, to interrupt the stifling silence inside their air-conditioned car. The husband slammed the steering wheel with a flat hand, and said. "Oh! I can't be doin' with this!" He spun the car about at the next tollbooth, and pointed it toward home. They passed almond trees bursting with pink and white blossoms. The girl said, "The darker the bloom, the more bitter the nut," and held one hand in the other to stop herself from slapping a mosquito crawling up her husband's forehead.

The girl picks up the sports section of the *Sunday Times*, grainy with sand, but after a page of cricket and red cards in football she sets it aside. A naked child squats facing the rows of umbrellas and sunbathers and has a straining poo as if performing in a talent show. The child's father looks out to sea beside her, juggling five crimson balls.

Three Arabic-looking men play a game on the sand with two boards and carved wooden pieces. No sailboats. There are never any sailboats. Just a cruise ship far out on the horizon. The girl has never seen a sea without a sailboat. This fills her with alarm. Also, there is haze instead of sun. As if the world is dipped in skim milk. What does this mean? And there are thousands of feet on this beach — bony, fat-toed, heel-crusted, wrinkled feet, orange feet, blotchy red feet with white stripes, and here and there, a foot with a warped big toe. Beside her, the husband looks through binoculars, scanning the beach as if he were a member of CSIS or an avid birder. The girl doesn't think she can take any more feet.

The girl's husband rises and swings off down the beach. After a bit, he passes a neighbour, Mrs. Walmsey, sitting alone against a fence with her basketball stomach, buck teeth, and broken arm. Mrs. Walmsey is the only person for a hundred kilometres besides the girl's husband who knows the girl's name. She is thirty-seven years older than the girl, and seated on an enormous beach towel while her husband bobs in the sea. She waves at the girl's husband tramping by. "Hiya, Duncan!" she calls. The girl's husband technically has no problem with Mrs. Walmsey, but he prefers to clarify he has no need of anyone. He moves by her, his body bent forward, neck cranked away, as if earnestly acting out Time over Distance equals Work.

Mr. Walmsey held a knife to Mrs. Walmsey's throat one night earlier this week, then changed his mind and broke her arm. He gets naughty, Mrs. Walmsey says. She speaks to the girl, but Mrs. Walmsey's worn down and talks to anyone. The girl was crouched up on the roof in the middle of the night when the kerfuffle occurred. She was squatting on the cold tiles thinking about how their rooftop house is growing mould in seven corners and how her husband corrects her all day long.

Mrs. Walmsey told the girl that she and her husband agreed she broke her arm by slipping on the stairs. "Too much fire water," Mr. Walmsey says, and all the neighbours laugh. The girl told her husband what she heard up on the roof. "Aren't you something," her husband said, and stalked out of the room with his fast little steps. He stuck his head back in and said, "You'll last two minutes here, being the fucking expert."

If she complains, he says, "Why don't you get on that plane, mate, if you don't like it? I'll purchase the ticket myself. When do you want to go? Tomorrow?" The girl has asked him to stop drinking and he promises several times a week. Sometimes he rubs her arms and says, kindly, "I know you are suffering. I can't stand to see you suffer." Then he walks into the kitchen and fills his glass with one-third Orange Fanta, and two-thirds gin, in the belief that she can't tell the difference. This dilutes the colour and makes him go on yappy pontifications. Often by bedtime he is still talking as he crawls between the sheets, even though the girl is on the roof and can barely hear him calling angrily, "So you've never had zebra steak? I myself have visited Kenya and dined on zebra steak on four occasions . . ." From time to time, the husband apologizes. Yesterday, when he asked for the girl's forgiveness, crying, "I don't know what gets into me!" the girl said, "Jesus says we only have to forgive seventy times seven." This made her feel large and windblown.

Out to sea, a man is walking on the water, long hair flying.

A woman with a deeply burnt neckline and thighs comes down the beach, her large feet in sandals sinking in the sand. She has caught sight of the topless woman lying near the girl. "Fancy finding you here, Frances!" the burnt woman says, ploughing over. "We didn't think you holidayed. Ha ha." The topless woman lifts her arms, which makes her breasts look larger, and the girl sees her startling marble-veined underarms. The burnt woman slides her top off too, whumps down onto the sand, and tells the first woman that her daughter and the daughter's new husband are building a spectacular house in Manchester. She tells her topless acquaintance it has four baths, all with bidets. She tells her all about the two sitting rooms with textured wallpaper and fancy coving and chair railings. About the crystal chandelier that cost two thousand pounds, and the dining suite shipped all the way from London. She goes on about the English garden with nine different kinds of roses and a gazebo. "My daughter and her husband take twice yearly trips to Florida," the woman says. This is because the husband is a solicitor and so wealthy. The solicitor *begged* her daughter to marry him. Has she mentioned? The son-in-law has invited the burnt woman and her husband along on their next trip to America. "We get on so well," the burnt woman says, closing her eyes and smiling beatifically. The burnt woman would need two large dinner plates to hold her breasts. The girl is astounded at the size of breasts here. The burnt woman tells the topless one, whose nipples are staring angrily at the overhead sun, that in America people say samich. I'll have a hole whee samich. The topless woman's husband keeps his eyes closed through the entire conversation while his wife stretches her lips over her teeth and says, "Is that so? Is that so?"

When the burnt woman leaves, the topless one pokes her husband and says, "I'm not envious. Are you envious, Tom? I'm not envious!" She chomps down on a fried egg sandwich and glowers at her striped feet for a while and says, "I fail to see why you won't telephone Michelle."

"She hangs up," the woman's husband says without opening his eyes.

Mrs. Walmsey is smoking cigarettes farther down the beach. The girl imagines how it might feel to abandon someone. She imagines it feels like light. Mrs. Walmsey abandoned her son to live with Mr. Walmsey when the boy was ten. Twenty-one years ago. She told the girl this when Mrs. Walmsey was wet-mopping her outside stairs and the girl was standing in her own yard under the fig tree, doing nothing. There is nothing here to do. Then nine years ago Mrs. Walmsey disowned the son all over again for being gay. "It were Slim's idea. He don't get on with 'arry." Mrs. Walmsey ground out her half-smoked cigarette and laid it carefully on the wheelbarrow. She picked her way across the garden pebbles to their adjoined fence and blew smoke out. "He never did take to 'arry, but now, on account he's flaming queer, Slim won't give him time o' day." The British here leave the articles out of their sentences. "Let's go pub." "We'll go in car." These people speak like toddlers! the girl thinks. Mrs. Walmsey tied her shoe, and stood up fast as if to catch the girl at something. "Don't tell nobody, Donna. You're different, like the last one, so I'm tellin' ya. People here get wind?! Obviously." Mrs. Walmsey blew out her cheeks. The girl smelled damp newspapers. "I got cause not to speak to 'arry. He's been falsely telling his mate — t'one he shacked up with — he were brought up in a cardboard box." Mrs. Walmsey bent in a hacking cough. "Bloke telephoned from London see what were fact. Cheeky. It were only playpen I could afford. I put him in cereal aisle while I were on till. I could see him. He had his toys an' all. He likes to stir the pot, 'arry. Turned queer to put me off."

"Watch your bum!" Mr. Walmsey will say if he hears

Harry's name. This makes the girl's husband laugh. "Good bloke, Slim," he'll say and then the two of them sit on Mr. Walmsey's steps and have another beer.

"Are all Canadians mucky buggers then?" Mrs. Walmsey has asked, because the girl never washes her stairs, doesn't spend each morning scrubbing down her cupboards, but Mrs. Walmsey cackles her smoky laugh, "so it won't be took wrong way." She tells the girl that cleanliness and order are what keep a country from wrack and ruin. "Me mum saved bags she bought her tea cakes in, tidied straight and folded. All in fine piles in kitchen drawers. Take away school uniforms and you have anarchy. Obviously," Mrs. Walmsey says.

Down the beach the girl's husband is growing small, shooting up sprays of sand behind his receding heels. Over on her large beach towel, Mrs. Walmsey lights another cigarette and waves. A few metres away, a woman throws her drink in a man's face. A clump of men move by, old skin hanging. Salt prickles the girl's nostrils. She closes her eyes and pictures Moorish gardens: orange, lemon, níspero, apricot trees, figs, and pomegranates. The backs of her eyelids burst with the colour saffron.

The girl lies flat on her back under the umbrella, which gives small shrieks in the breeze. Jesus walks the roadway, gathering material from construction sites, favouring thick strips of plastic tenting he picks out of the air. The last time the girl and her husband drove up-country, they stopped for a picnic at the edge of a ravine two hours north, past Coveta Fuma. Across the sharp-plunging valley, a cave town climbed the mountain. But when the girl peered over the ravine's edge, she saw a humungous dump: rubble, dirt, lumps of stone and refuse strewn down the near side of the hill. Dented refrigerators, cracked televisions, mattress springs, micro-waves, washing machines, building plastics, drinking cups, crunched-up chocolate wrappers lifting in the wind, rolling bottles. As if a gigantic garbage truck had had an accident.

The girl exclaimed, "This is the view the people in the cave town are graced with!"

"Must it always be about you?" her husband said.

The girl digs her legs and bottom into the hot, hot sand and thinks of the melted coke bottles you can buy at the market, necks crooked like elbows.

Mrs. Walmsey, in her violet-flowered bathing suit, is walking toward the girl, pulling on a cigarette. "Hiya, Donna," she says and sits down on the husband's beach towel. "Headache," she says after a while. She reaches round the back of her head with her good hand to show the girl a bald patch. "Slim ripped me hair out. He were funny again last night." She touches above her ear. "Sore all way t'here." The girl can see Mr. Walmsey, bobbing in the sea.

"It don' take much for Slim to get funny. But this morning din' he go and want to take me swimming, put it right. It's the anniversary of me mum's death and I am upset I had to go to shops and go about with no bra on on 'count of me useless arm. I just broke down. But then I had me some nice rice pudding what calms me. My arthritis is acting up in me good wrist. I'm tellin' you on account of I know you was hiding up on roof t'other night. I don't care for the sea. Never learned to swim. I were never able to close me mouth on account o' me buck teeth. Obviously." Then, "You know that woman what recently took up with Bert?"

Who is Bert? The girl's neighbours are just faces to her.

"Well, she's fifty-four come October. She went and had boob job and then din' one nipple up and die. Wednesday, not fortnight later, off dropped t'other—like raisin—in sink." Mrs. Walmsey lights another cigarette. "And Malcolm got new elbow and din' it fuse! Sticks out as if 'e's about to shake hands. Isn't the forecast just gloom and doom!" Mrs. Walmsey rubs the ashes on her bathing suit into a messy triangle.

"Hiya," she says after a while when the girl's husband returns. The husband nods in all directions but at the girl.

"Where did you go?" the girl asks when Mrs. Walmsey leaves.

Her husband cracks another beer. Jesus and Salvador Dalí have hang-glided into an ancient palm grove in Elche, and are strolling, picking dates, and discussing whether Christopher Columbus's body travelled more before his death or after. Issac Albéniz is following behind, complaining of kidney pain.

"I'm feeling peckish for jacket potatoes," the husband says. "But I expect you don't know how to prepare them properly."

"Death rates caused by alcohol are up forty-five per cent," the girl reads aloud from a section of the *Sunday Times*.

The look the husband gives her!

The girl imagines disappearing. Going underground. Forgetting to wash her hair. Finding a seedy hotel where she could remain just one more mystery in a draughty smoke-filled room.

When she wasn't married by twenty-one, the girl's mother conjured up a dead air force pilot for her. Told the mother's friends who came to drink strong tea and eat her thawed-out lemon squares, "Such a tragedy. Donna can't get over the man. Arthur was crazy about her. His parents were from Tennessee. His mother descended from French aristocracy. Ar-toor, they called him. Ar-toor adored Donna . . ." Her mother values the non-existent and the dead, who can be put to use.

The girl is sick to death of ham. All you can buy in the shops is canned tuna, fish, and ham. And the electricity keeps going off.

"These lights are as useless as Canadian lights," her husband declares each time they blink out.

"But you returned to Canada. You must like things about it," the girl sometimes presses. Her husband says, "How could I return to England?" This the girl understands.

She checks her messages. She has no messages. She closes her eyes and pictures Sunday, the only adult she has ever known who never lost her baby teeth.

She listens to the waves, which become the sound of skipping rhymes, the faint slap-slap of the rope.

CHRIS-topher Co-LUMbus was a VE-ry brave MAN,
He SAILED 'cross the O-cean in an OLD tin CAN!
The waves grew higher, and HIGHer and OVER!

The waves make designs in the sand that look like a wasp's nest. The girl imagines Antoni Gaudí's Casa Milà, the movement of waves across a stone façade.

She lies in the grit and thinks of ivory fans, of carved cedar, of ebony, onyx, alabaster, of mosaic tiles and marble columns. She thinks of the famous knight, El Cid, and his jewelled belt, the *al-thu'ban,* the snake. For a wedding gift, the girl bought her husband cufflinks at Swarovski, a little snake curled in their centre.

"Swarovski!" the man who is her husband said. "Well, it's no Mappin and Webb!"

For his birthday, she presented him with an old black box imprinted with a map of the world she'd found in the antique store in Salmon Arm. "Antique! You people don't know the meaning of old. I can buy Roman coins in York that date back to the fourth century! You play at life like you play checkers," he added irritably. "You are unable to take in the whole board."

The girl's mother used to find it a joke to stick straight pins into the dish rag, for the pleasure of watching her father shriek when he wrung it out.

An animal scuttles by in the tall dune grasses behind the girl. She wonders if Spain has opossums. She did a report on opossums in school. She knows everything about opossums. The young live on their mothers' backs for months. Their hind foot is actually a hand. The females have a double uterus and a double vagina and the males have a forked penis. Her world is full of information that does her no good.

"Arabic words are fluid," the girl says to her husband who pretends to sleep. "They change shape depending on their placement within the sentence." Her husband starts lightly snoring. A wind blows over him. Usually he smells like furniture polish and foreign cologne. On some days he smells like dragon fruit gone rank. Or devilled eggs. Or sinkholes. The girl believes he is rotting from the inside.

Arabic letters grace the porticoes of the Alhambra in Granada. Her father described them to her until the girl knows them by heart. The letters curl and dip behind her closed eyelids. A peacock wanders through the palace and comes upon the court calligrapher setting out his tools: his *cálamo* ink pen; beside it, his knife to sharpen the cálamo; and his pot of ink whose dark colour comes from burnt wool and gum; and his strip of silk to apply ink to the cálamo. The calligrapher sweeps curved lines in Nastaliq, like the shapes in the peacock's tail.

The husband wakes up and has a swim. Jesus wanders a narrow street in Valladolid, carrying under his arm a doll-house full of little nuns all screaming in Arabic, leaning back in ecstasy, wee arms reaching.

When the husband returns the girl asks, "Why do you never let me pack my own suitcase?"

The husband opens another beer and says, "Your methods are higgledy-piggledy."

When they packed for their honeymoon to Vancouver, the husband laid a pair of trousers on the bed and smoothed them flat. The girl folded a blouse in half and laid it inside the suitcase.

"No! No!" Her husband sped around the bed. Sometimes the girl pictures him as a cycle in the wash, circling furiously on Spin. "Trousers on the bottom! This creates fewer creases. Just go and read your book."

The girl gets so many things wrong. She wolfs her food, while her husband eats elegantly, in order to *savour*. He chews eighty times per mouthful. He taps out each chew with his fork.

The husband's first ex-wife still telephones if she wants money, or if the son has shoplifted. Her sharp voice careens down the wire. Sometimes the husband lays the receiver down, walks to the fridge and pours himself a gin and tonic. He uses the bathroom, grabs an imported chocolate bar from the basket on the counter, and picks up a magazine before returning. The woman hullabaloos on. This used to make the girl laugh. Now she realizes the husband married her to show the first ex-wife that he could get a young woman, and to parade her about the Costa Blanca villas. When they first arrived on the Costa Blanca, the husband said, "No, no! This isn't Canada! People here show cleavage!" and bought seven revealing lace-edged halter tops to decorate her small pert breasts, but this only put their neighbours off and caused him to fly at her, calling her a slapper. Sometimes, when he's been drinking, he sets her down to listen while he lists the admirable qualities of his previous wives, who did not embarrass him in public; his last, despite being Canadian, could make perfect leek and potato soup.

"Do you know of the virtues of Motadid's son?" the girl asks the husband as he towels off. "When one of his wives longed for the sight of snow, he planted thousands of almond trees on a nearby slope so that each winter she might enjoy a white sea of blossoms." After a bit the girl says, "Such were the Moors." And when the husband doesn't answer, "Would you like to share my umbrella?" He has turned a frightful shade of red.

"I don't want anything from you," the husband says.

The girl cracks the spine of her second book, but the sun is skidding down the sky. The waves are blackening. It is becoming difficult to see. She says, "This story is about a wealthy older man at a pool party. He imagines his neighbours' pools spreading across the countryside. He imagines himself an explorer. He goes home by swimming through every pool between the party house and his own."

Her husband shakes his head, digs in his ears, shakes out his beach towel, and packs the papers in their sack.

"The landscape begins to change. The leaves blight. He finds his friends at each poolside increasingly hostile. A storm blows in. The man becomes confused."

The husband starts tramping toward the car.

"He reaches home at last, cold, aching, and half drowned," the girl calls. "His house is dark. The shutters dangle. The door is locked. He tries to force it. Finally he stands on tiptoe and looks in the little square of window, and he sees that the place is deserted, his family long ago departed."

The girl yanks the umbrella from the sand, picks up the beach bag, and follows her husband.

"Let's go to Córdoba," she calls. Córdoba, the place of kings, of conquistadors and saints. The capital of Moorish Spain. Gardens, petal-filled patios and arcing fountains. *Lejos,* the girl thinks. Far. *En breve:* Soon. *Bastante:* Enough. *Finalmente:* Finally. *Despertar:* To wake up. *Perder:* To lose. *Olvidar:* To forget. *Faltar:* To fail.

The husband guns the car into the encroaching night.

The girl slips through Córdoba's pebbled streets, glides across the Alfonso Bridge. Out of the darkness a speckled Arabian blue-white horse stands crossways on the bridge. He whinnies, lifting the white hollow of his throat. Across the water, the wail of the *canto jondo* and his flamenco guitar. As the girl approaches, the horse stamps once, and lowers his head to touch his nostrils to the tin can at his feet. The girl drops in a coin. Near the horse, a man in strappy sandals, with flowing sandy hair under a fedora, and the blackest of eyes, leans against the stone bridge wall, smoking.

Below, the Guadalquivir River murmurs milky green. A tree rises from the river, dressed in white birds.

In Which
Floyd's Odometer
Surpasses the
Million Kilometre
Mark and Friends
and Acquaintances
Reduce Their
Clutter:
A Milesian Tale

Thwacker[1]

Floyd bends stiff knees and creaks open the rusty water spigot in Roslyn's back yard. He is scrubbing his paint-brushes when the neighbour, Con, who's been in his back yard all afternoon, babysitting his helmeted daughter and watching Floyd work, pokes his head over the fence. "Floyd! Time to wrap her up, goddamn it. Come on over for a beer!"

---

1   A funnel-shaped device where the ball enters at the wide top and spins to the narrow bottom.

"There in a jiffy!" Floyd shouts back, and the two of them bullshit and drink while Ruby careens around on her tricycle, yahooing, chased by the farting dog.

One drink turns into four.

At three p.m. Floyd fires off a jovial goodbye, kisses the kid, gives the dog a squeeze, and feeling positively fertile with friendship, locks up Roslyn's house, loads his mitre saw and tools into the back of his truck and rattles out of Calgary. He cruises the three-hour, fifty-seven minute drive through the windy Crowsnest Pass, truck pointed toward his acreage, which skirts the village of Jaffray, crooning along to the oldie-goldies: "Under the Boardwalk," "Good Vibrations," "Summertime Blues." Semis hurtle past him as he weaves the solid lines.

Just twenty minutes from home, Floyd pulls into Fernie for a beer (turns into three) at the war-time house with no basement that he rents to his pal Kouzie. Floyd refurbished the place years back with spare parts scrounged from houses he was working on, including his own. His wife — his first — would walk into their pantry to stow the broom behind the closet door, and find the door gone. Around that time Floyd came home one afternoon and found his wife gone. Heart cracked like leather. But hey, shit happens. Floyd lets Kouzie live in the house in exchange for keeping up the yard and servicing Floyd's truck.

Floyd and Kouzie go way back: high school buddies who organized a betting ring on ping-pong tournaments noon hours in the cluttered room behind the stage. Kouzie never got over his high school sweetheart, Sylvia, who, he has confided to Floyd, still makes him want to stuff her down his shirt. For the last six months, Roslyn's occupied Floyd's head. "She's a doll," Floyd tells Kouzie each time he stops in after another job at Roslyn's house. "She's got this twisty cowlick, and pretty laugh lines, and that little gap between her teeth. Turns a guy's heart inside out. Sweet little thing can't change a light bulb." One day Kouzie, daydreaming of Sylvia, cut off his index finger with the tile setter. That stubby appendage jerked him to his senses. Now he works as an automotive painter, and sleeps with a sensible woman everybody calls Screech, who runs the welder fabrication shop across from Mug Shots Bistro.

Floyd's friends pour out their troubles to him, and their friends' troubles too. Stories trail Floyd like the clouds of exhaust chasing his dinged-up tailpipe. He just listens, rubbing his ear. "Yup," he'll say. Or, "Gotta do what you can at the pinball machine of life." Or "Anything to keep the ball from careening down the drain."

Floyd leaves Kouzie sitting in his garage, smiling, surrounded by car parts and beer, and arrives home in Jaffray. Wednesday, August 3rd. 8:53 p.m.

The Backbox[2]

Wednesday afternoon. August 3rd, 3:32 p.m. Roslyn traipses along Vancouver streets. Day two of a quick holiday to visit Stella who moved to Vancouver three months ago after

---

2   The backbox portion of the table serves two purposes: to hold the main electronics of the game, and to attract players.

meeting Blinky online. This is it, Stella said on the telephone. This one's the real McCoy. Come down and meet him. Of course Blinky flew the coop before Roslyn could board the plane. But why waste a ticket? A faint circle of early moon clings to the summer sky. Roslyn's worries peeling away like husbands, explosions of happiness zinging her arms. She's wearing the button she found at the flea market yesterday. *The first two husbands were just for practice.* But truth be told, she's through with being suction-cupped to a man. Hot sunlight licks her legs, reaching through the arbutus trees, red wood peeled back to a greenish-silver satin sheen.

Roslyn stops at the corner shop showcasing blueberries piled deep in glass drawers, and buys a bag for Stella. She passes on the pistachios piled on the counter. Stella doesn't chew nuts. She aspirates them.

By the time Roslyn reaches the bottom of Stella's front stairs, she's sticky with heat, envisions a cool afternoon shower before Stella gets home from work. Roslyn climbs the steep steps to the tall narrow house. A rustling through the open window. Doesn't Stella's shift end at five?

"Stella?"

A whispered, "Goddamn!" A whispered, "Go." Squelch-ings. Giggles. Wet slap-slapping. Frantic crescendoed breath-ing. Roslyn, for all her resole, climbs on, rides, bucking the flotsam and jetsam of Stella's lust. A cartoon rises in her brain: an excited pencil sharpener, handle whirring, shav-ings flying in all directions.

"Yee*haw!*" Stella hollers from the living room.

The front door swings open a minute later to reveal a shirt-less man fanning himself with a cooking pot. "Hi, Eileen!"

"Roslyn, Splasho!" Stella calls. *"Roslyn!"*

Roslyn yanks at her damp shirt and steps inside. Stella appears beside Splasho, deodorant streaks across the breast of her cocktail dress from the careless way she's yanked it on. "Roslyn. This is Splasho. Sorry." She gives Roslyn a sweaty hug. "We thought we had till five." Stella pins a floating strand of hair with a bobby pin, waves a hand, and Roslyn follows them deeper into the house, ambrosial sunshine spilling through the skylight. Down on the street a little boy not more than three stands, mouth open wide in indignant soundless crying, holding a cone before him like a microphone, a splat of violet ice cream perched between his toes, a slug of it crawling off his foot.

Splasho grabs his T-shirt, which has flung itself across the stove, wipes his forehead with it, swipes his chest, grins at Roslyn, and gallantly pulls out two chairs at Stella's fake oak kitchen table as if he and Stella weren't, mere moments ago, tangled in something intimate, messy, and urgent. He opens his jaw and works it, works it. From the street comes an enraged exhaled roar.

"Splasho's mouth gets stuck open after sex," Stella says.

Splasho is *so* not Blinky, and a good thing too. Two brief Skype calls to Stella and Blinky had revealed a pot-belly, a fringe of hair, and no ability to small talk. Even so, just last night, Roslyn had to listen to the story, word by clenched-out word, Roslyn perched on the toilet seat, Stella hunkered in the tub, scraping her skin with an exfoliating glove. How Blinky left Stella twenty-seven days ago for Valerie, who works in a soap shop on Robson Street. Blinky, holding a bottle of mango lotion, 240 mls, and examining a sponge from the Congo that promised tantalizing, never-before-imagined uses — birthday gifts for Stella — when all that perfume overcame him in a dizzy spell. How he fell against a promotional pile of foot lotions on the way down. How Valerie dropped the customer she was lecturing on the benefits of heel scrubs, hauled Blinky to the back room, and his revival progressed from there. And everything got a second wind. His breathing, his colour, his dong.

"Want one of my brownies?" Stella plunks a plastic container of brown lumps on the table.

"I would personally love that," Splasho says, tapping a cigarette out of its pack. "Who does not love Stella's baked goods? Unfortunately, I'm allergic to cocoa."

"There's an article on tact in *GQ*," Stella says. "Shall I cut it out for you?"

She reaches around Splasho, grabs a brownie, and sets about rearranging her cupboards according to the tenets of feng shui in a magazine article she's laid out on the table. Free your life of clutter and your fortunes will run smooth as water. Stella points out the importance of order as she works, things placed just so: cereal boxes, spice jars, herbal teas, vinegars. "And it's imperative"— she whizzes a lid-crusted jar of fish sauce into the garbage can —"to check Best Before dates. Chuck anything ready to expire."

"I have," Roslyn says. "It's why I'm single."

Splasho laughs. "Well, if you need an occasional tune-up—"

"Go screw yourself, Splasho," Stella says cheerfully.

Splasho, still chuckling, shoves back his chair, "I'm outa here." He clomps across the floor in his dusty dingo boots, and roars off on his motorcycle.

"Roslyn, you haven't rehung that big mirror in your bedroom now that Floyd's redone it, have you?" Stella's head disappears in the hall closet. Her voice is echo-y. "Well, for god's sake, take it down! It's bad feng shui."

Friday evening, August 5th. 11:59 p.m. Roslyn descends from the plane at the Calgary International Airport after a choppy flight in which flight attendants on WestJet smiled wide, disconcerting smiles, and winked over-exaggerated winks, the open-mouthed kind, and laughed hard at their own jokes while running the cart up and down the aisles to see if people wanted to pay $3.69 for a tiny plastic bag of pretzels with the salt crumbled in one corner.

Roslyn catches a taxi from the airport. Her eager driver, having just returned from Italy, takes his corners like European roundabouts. He clamps to a stop outside Roslyn's almost-renovated house, and she stumbles from the taxi feeling she's seeing through a crystal wine glass. She staggers up her steps, drops her suitcase and carry-on in her bedroom, takes a look at herself in her bad-feng-shui mirror, and clacks down the stairs to see how Floyd's coming with the wainscoting, if he's painted the laundry room yet, or laid the tiles on her workout room floor. She steps off the second bottom step into a foot of water. Clean water. This she discovers by snapping on the light, white purse clutched against her stomach like a stranded cat. No floating feces, no plum pits, no mouldy banana peels. The washer and dryer shine eerily in water that laps like polite applause. Roslyn stands mid-calf in the pool. She pictures baptism. She pictures redemption. She pictures Gene Kelly tap dancing to "Singing in the Rain."

The splashy leap, heels clicked above the flood. Upstairs the phone rings, muffled jangles. After five rings it stops.

Roslyn opens a door. A toothpick bobs by. She sloshes up the hallway, into her storage room, then her workout room with its partially-submerged exercise bike and stepper, the room where the previous owners left a second fridge. It's grinding ominously. Water licks her ankles as if tasting her.

Roslyn squelches upstairs, leaving amphibian footprints and stands on the landing, her mind a murky lake. A gurgling reaches her ears. She opens the back door. The garden hose is splashing gaily against the house foundation. A homeless couple rattles a Safeway cart past in the alley.

Roslyn shuts off the tap, dries her feet on the landing rug, climbs the three steps up to her kitchen and checks the phone. A 1-800 number. She crawls into bed and leans at half-mast against her pillows, chilled feet propped, stuffing her face with tissue-flecked raspberry licorice from the bottom of her purse, and trying not to gag.

Saturday, August 6th. 6:09 a.m. Roslyn rises and brushes her teeth, licorice bits sticking to her toothbrush like disintegrating gums. She descends to the basement. The water is still there, lapping against the washing machine. She climbs back upstairs and dials Floyd's number.

"Top o' the marning to you!" Floyd says.

"Floyd. Did you leave the outside tap running when you left my house on Wednesday?"

"Well, fuck," Floyd says.

"Because my basement has a foot of water in it."

"Oh my fuck," Floyd says.

The Playfield[3]

Saturday, August 6th. 7:02 a.m. Floyd perches on his easy chair under his deer heads, downing glasses of homemade plum wine to slow his heart rate. Jesus fucking Christ. He'll bring her something. Last night he killed a goose. Rendered the fat. Took him till three a.m. He'll bring her a jar of goose lard. Two tablespoons in a cup of boiled milk. Cures any ailment. Better than a flu shot. That and a bag of his home-made beef jerky. Roslyn *relies* on him for Chrissakes. She has a way of getting him to tell her things. How his second ex moved out and into the very women's shelter he'd built in town less than a year before — no rent, and convenient for banging the town cop. How he considered buying an escort agency with Tuff Novakosky in the seventies, but the deal fell through. Roslyn would give him her straight gaze and he'd duck out to the garage thinking, Why the hell did I go and tell her *that?!* But then he'd look at her tight little body and her sweet small feet, and he'd open his mouth and tell her another damn thing.

Floyd sits under his deer heads, deep-breathing. He loves Roslyn, he loves the hell out of that woman, and now he's fucked it all to pieces. He empties the bottle. He pulls a beer from the fridge. Then he starts in on the homemade Baileys his grow-op neighbour on the acreage across gave him at

---

3   The pinball playfield is inclined at a six to seven degree angle toward the player, creating a hill on which the ball is influenced by gravity just enough to speed it along through the obstacles.

Christmas even though he's lactose intolerant. Well, he'll just have to fix the mess.

Floyd paces his rec room, drops a nervous coin in the pinball machine he salvaged from the Jaffray dump. It flashes *Press Start*. Floyd punches the button, and the flippers whack, whack, whack, the pinball flying, Floyd propelling it up the bumpers and ramps. Clunk. The ball drops down the drain.

Floyd has one more shot of Baileys for the road, steps out and feeds the deer who are impatiently pawing his deck —hungry, though they stand on their hind legs all goddamn day and pick plums off his trees, then trail deer crap across his lawn. Floyd gets in his truck and drives across the border to Eureka, Montana, where gas is cheaper. So are supplies. He steps into Lucky Lil's on Main. Saturday morning. 9:25. No one in the joint. Floyd takes a table by the open door. Orders a beer. Is fishing for quarters at the juke box when two men walk in and scrape back chairs at the table next to Floyd's. Big mother-fuckers. "All My Ex's Live in Texas," George Strait wails. The one is shaved bald, the other has a Mohawk. Every time Floyd looks up, Mohawk is staring at him. Floyd nods. He walks back to his table and sits down. He'd like to take a different table, but his beer is sitting on this one. Mohawk raises his fists. "These mothers are registered with the NYPD!"

His partner, without pulling his eyes from the Manchester United football match on the television screen, says, "He's not lying."

Floyd takes a polite sip.

"Got these anger issues." The man scrapes his feet on the

peanut-shelled floor. "Goddamn brother's getting married and who'd he ask to be fucking best man? Not me."

Floyd licks chapped lips. "Problem I have is getting the right woman to the altar," he says.

The man clenches his thighs.

Floyd makes sympathetic noises; then, when the silence swells, clears his throat, bends over and takes another sip. His mind keeps flitting to Roslyn's basement. He'll have to rent a water vacuum and water pump from Servpro. Put those giant dryers in. A thousand bucks. At least.

"I was so pissed off I had to . . ." Barcelona scores and the crowd lets out a roar.

"You had to what?" Floyd hauls his chair forward. He's deaf at the best of times. "— climb a *tree?*"

The man glowers. "Retreat! I had to GO TO A RETREAT!" He leans forward, splays large hands, one on Floyd's table, one on his own. Presses. "Learn to channel my anger." He's breathing through his nose.

Well, Jesus Christ. Floyd buys them all a round.

"You seem like a nice person," Mohawk says after they all drink. "Real open. Real uncorrupted by the darkness. Where you from?"

"Up over the border," Floyd says. He runs his tongue over his teeth. "Canada."

The man snaps his fingers, does a gonna-getcha-finger-point. "Thaswhy!" And out the door he strides. Baldie gets up and follows, neck cranked back at the game. Floyd finishes his beer, downs two more to slow his heart rate, and heads for the lumber store: drywall, insulation, tape, vapour barrier, lots of nails.

He loads his truck and calls Roslyn on his cell. No answer so he leaves a message.

Hi good lookin'. Hi doll. Just down in Eureka picking up a few supplies. I'll rent a water vacuum and a water pump when I hit Calgary, and we'll suck that lake up. 11:03 now. Be there by six o'clock tonight. Keep that pretty smile on. Yeah. Floyd here.

Nudge [4]

Saturday, August 6th. 10:35 a.m. Kouzie sits at the breakfast table eating yesterday's leftover smoked chicken and artichoke pizza, eyes flitting over his sticky notes of clients' addresses, jokes ripped from *Reader's Digest*, and *Playboy* pin-up girls taped to his cupboard doors. He looks at Miss August and thinks of Sylvia. The way she stuffed her bra in high school, crying when the wads of Kleenex fell out on the floorboards of his Buick at the drive-in.

His mother is sitting in his living room, in his La-Z-Boy chair, feet up, glued to yesterday's soaps, which she insisted Kouzie tape, fake eyelashes bobbing about her sunken eyes as she watches Earl steal Melissa's baby and Roberto head off to jail for a crime of passion.

Kouzie sticks the last two pizza pieces in a plastic bag, along with a bagel and a wrinkled apple. Adds a Red Bull. If his mother wasn't filling Kouzie's house with her upsetting feelings, or standing on his small back deck, grinding

---

4   A method of trying to control the ball by moving the machine itself.

through her cigarettes, Kouzie would trot back home for lunch. But he'd rather eat perched on a car part than listen to her gripe.

From what he can piece together, his mother's boyfriend, Duck, stayed in Arizona, getting some on the side from an old dame, Ardythe, who his mother knows from Thursday bingo in Vernon, and who, according to his mother, has been caught twice cheating at pegs and jokers.

"Ardythe, now there's a desperate woman," Kouzie's mother calls, as if Ardythe has suddenly appeared on the television screen. She chomps grimly on her breakfast dessert from Big Bang Bagels, cream cheese hanging off her lip. She rises suddenly and smokes, white waves fogging back through the open sliding doors. "She has it something awful." She raises her voice, now that she is technically in the back yard, though she's only three feet from Kouzie's table. The mountains loom behind her in angry Vs. "Cutting in at dances! Buying those giant cookies from the Paradise Vice Bakery and pretending she baked them. You can tell!" His mother lays her burning cigarette on the deck, steps in, rips off a piece of paper towel, steps back out, wipes her fingers and picks up the smouldering cigarette. "I had no choice but to get on a plane — it was that or sleep three in a bed in Duck's trailer. I have my principles," his mother sniffs.

Kouzie's hand is on the door.

"He knows my Vernon house is rented till the end of September. I may have to stay with you till fall, Clarence. I'll fix your favourite — my cheese whiz meatloaf for supper. Bye sweetie," his mother says.

Kouzie hasn't been at work much over an hour when Floyd sticks his head in the shop door.

"Odometer just passed the million-kilometre mark," Floyd sings. "Heading to Calgary. Brought you plums. It's that or let the deer shit themselves to death." Floyd disappears and comes back with a microwave box full of purple plums. "Got a few toilet paper rolls handy?" Floyd says.

Kouzie cracks two beer.

"Thought you might be rolling back this direction some time soon," Kouzie says. "She's a pretty lady, sound of it."

Floyd busies himself shoving papers around Kouzie's desk and sets down his beer can.

"I figure you just might be scheming up some make-work projects," Kouzie says. "Could be doing her odd jobs for years."

Floyd ducks his head and drinks. "I've half a mind to ask her on a trip to Europe, Kouzie. She lived there. She could show me around. I'd like to know how those old buildings were constructed."

Kouzie leans against a bumper. "Maybe think about rolling your odometer back, Floydo. You'll make more when you sell her."

Floyd rubs his ear. "I'm bringing her goose lard. I ever tell you? 1913 my father was bedridden for a year in the old country. TB. Cold, chest pains, laryngitis, coughing. During the course of time a caravan of gypsies came through the village. Gypsy woman gave my father a cup of boiled milk with goose lard." He shakes his head. "Healed the bugger."

Wind sweeps in the open doorway, fluttering Kouzie's pin-up of Virginia Bell.

"Got some elk tongue in my freezer," Floyd says after a while. "Had one last night on the barbecue. Good with hot mustard. Come down some night, Kouzie, and I'll cook you one."

"Could we go for supper at the Legion tonight, Floydo?" Kouzie says. "Mother's making her cheese whiz meatloaf."

Replay[5]

Sunday, August 7th. 11:00 a.m. Stella, vacuum cleaner cord in hand, looks out at the dogwood tree bent under a tattoo of grey rain. Two days since Splasho hightailed. Hopped on his machine and roared out of town. Stella's eye is starting up again. Aching prickly pain. She walked to Casa Gelato on Prior yesterday morning, and was mugged by a shaky guy who dodged sideways around the back of the auto shop, and snatched the wallet Stella had pulled from her purse to recheck for her credit card, which she is prone to leaving behind in shops. He got in one punch. Could swing but he couldn't run. Stella chased and tackled. Got her wallet. And one black eye.

A racket sounds down on the street at the bottom of Stella's steps. She swings open her front door. There stand a drenched Adelaide and Irvin, trying to negotiate their paraphernalia, which includes a suitcase, a brightly-wrapped package, and a cake.

---

5   The pinball flies around the table. If it doesn't hit your bumpers and targets to score points, it eventually falls down the drain and you move on to your next ball.

"Adelaide!"

"Happy birthday!" her sister hollers, and she and Irvin start puffing up the gauntlet of steps. "We got up at three-thirty this morning. Drove all the way from Salmon Arm." Adelaide clatters ahead, bumping their small cases and bags. "Brakes were going," Adelaide puffs, "due to all the hills in town. You know how Irvin likes to ride the brake." They stop on the steps and have an argument in the driving rain about whether to get the brakes fixed in Vancouver or risk the trip home. Irvin feels loyal to Bart's Muffler in Salmon Arm. Bart's Muffler brings in mufflers from China, but Bart does brakes on the side. "Hudson Avenue," Irvin tells Stella, his face dripping. "Just down from the post office."

"Nobody gives a rat's ass what street it's on, Irvin," Adelaide says over her shoulder.

Eventually they reach the top. Adelaide collapses onto the ottoman. Stella walks about the living room, picking up their summer sweaters, which stink of wet wool, and putting them on hangers.

"Conversely, Stella cares that I get home without being hurtled off a mountain road. Irvin's always driving with one hand, off in la-la land, digging in the glove compartment, fidgeting with the air vents. Here. Happy Birthday."

"A nail buffer," Stella says, opening the package. "And leather pants." She holds them up.

"Not *leather!*" Adelaide says. "Spandex and cotton. Good for cellulite. The leather *look*. $19.99 in Buggerbee's Clothing Emporium clearout section." Adelaide heaves off her perch and pushes Irvin down the hall with his suitcase and the shopping bags. "Eighty per cent off," she says. "I sniff out deals, Stella, like you sniff out useless men. Do we get to meet Splasho? What? Why? No, don't answer. I don't want to know. Here, let me finish your vacuuming. No, I insist. We've been sitting for six hours. Any more and we'll form blood clots." Irvin is already back in the living room parked on Stella's couch, watching a rerun of *Favourite World Cup Playoffs* he recorded and brought along. Adelaide pokes the vacuum under his feet.

"You don't choose trustworthy ones," Adelaide says loudly over the vacuum's whir. "You need to pick someone like Irvin. Don't even consider dating again, Stella, unless you check with Irvin and me. Phone if you feel yourself succumbing. We'll drive right down."

Stella sits at her kitchen table and has a cup of tea with the birthday cake Adelaide picked up at the Union Street Market. The icing is rain-sogged. Stella scrapes it off. The sound of the vacuum's motor mixes with the thrum of rain, reminding her of her new nail buffer. She read in an article at the hairdresser's that nail buffers have dual benefits. Though she'll have to remember, the article said, to set it on low. Tonight. A little birthday present to herself.

Late that afternoon, Stella is chewing a handful of Brazil nuts and hanging the faux-leather pants in her closet while watching snippets of *Oprah* through the open doorway. The phone rings.

"A flood, Roslyn!" Stella says. "Floyd did? Well, you should take him out for dinner. The man's done you a service. No, forget insurance. Roslyn, focus! The universe is speaking. It's calling you to balance your living space. Clean up your environs. Only then will insurance feel the positive vibes and pay." Stella coughs, aspirates, carries on. "The flood? It's the cosmos reaching out to tell you. Roslyn! It's feng shui! Tidy your house and your life will follow. Floyd's done the renos. Now the universe is—Ooooh! Gives me the willies! Roslyn! What direction is your bed facing? West?! Holy shit. And your bedroom doorway? West? God, girl. That's the death position! Feet first out the door. No wonder the place is heaving up. Get in there right now, *right now* Roslyn, and shove your bed to the other wall. I'll wait."

Stella watches Oprah admiring Dr. Oz, who is telling women the secret to healthy kidneys. Stella chews until Roslyn comes back on the phone.

"Storage boxes? You store boxes under your bed? Roslyn! Dispose of them immediately. The clutter isn't allowing natural flow—I'll wait. Well, put Theo's report cards in a cupboard or something. Cart them to the garage. Just get that clutter out of your bedroom, Roslyn, before it blows."

Target[6]

Sunday, August 7th. 11:16 a.m. "Well, we can be glad it didn't rain for forty days." Floyd stands rooted in Roslyn's basement in his rubber boots. "We'd have to build an ark. Nuns taught me everything I know. I was their star pupil. Ask me anything. How old was Noah?"

---

6   The pinball flies around the table, hitting bumpers and targets to
    score points; at least, that's what is desired.

"I have no idea," Roslyn says.

"Six hundred. He was six hundred fucking years old," Floyd says. "And still begetting like a tom cat. The waters prevailed . . ." Floyd turns on a machine, water burbles and sprays the dryer. He turns it off again. "Used to be an altar boy. The nuns loved me." He bends over the machine, adjusting something. There is a gurgle and a suck. "My favourite?" Floyd says, sloshing over to Roslyn. "Funerals. Got fifty cents for serving Communion and the afternoon off school!"

"How will you get all the water out with that little machine?"

"Don't you worry your pretty little head about it. We've got things under control." Floyd sloshes back across the laundry room. "We'll make a wind blow over the earth. What you got for fans?"

Roslyn goes upstairs and commences pulling Duncan's long white hairs out of her burnt-orange sofa chair.

Early evening, when the water is sucked up and the fans gusting, Floyd sits Roslyn down at her dining room table and presents her with goose lard. "Cures any ailment, even stress." He gets a mug out of her cupboard, fills it with milk and sets it in the microwave.

"What are you doing?" Roslyn says. "I can't drink that. I'd gag. I haven't drunk milk since I was five years old and the goose fat smells."

"Well, we'll make 'er chocolate," Floyd says. "Special treat for a special lady!" He rummages through Roslyn's cupboards, dumps two heaping teaspoons of cocoa in, adds a tablespoon of sugar, and starts up the microwave. He carries the milk to Roslyn as if it is a jewel; its surface glistening with golden pinpricks.

Everything's under control, Floyd tells Roslyn the following afternoon. Water sucked out. Fans humming. Basement drying. He'll be back in a matter of days. Enjoy the sunsets! He gets in his truck and clatters off.

Replay 2 [7]

Sunday, August 14th. 4:28 p.m. Roslyn is marking papers in her study when a woman with a British accent says accusingly, "Carbon monoxide poisoning. Leave the premises immediately."

Roslyn sticks her head into the hall.

The voice says it again, with urgency. It's coming from the detector Floyd installed in the hall. Roslyn steps outside and stands on her lawn, feeling foolish. She phones a city number on her cell and after a while a furnace van drives up.

"Carbon monoxide should be measuring sixty. It's reading four hundred," the furnace man says. "Furnace has to be shut down. I'm putting a tag on it. It's condemned. Stay out of the house for an hour till the gasses clear."

"Who'll pay for the new one?" Roslyn asks.

"You or insurance," the man says. "Not me! Ha ha."

---

7   When your third ball goes down the drain, your game is over, unless you've played well enough to score a replay.

Frenzy[8]

Thursday, August 18th. 9:13 a.m. A man begins to dismantle the furnace. Roslyn is cutting chunks of chilled butter into a mixture of flour and sugar for her Chocolate Blueberry Scones when the man leaps into the kitchen, tearing appliances out of their sockets as he runs, hollering, "Natural gas! Ma-am! Get the hell out! MOVE! Get off the steps! Get off the goddamn steps! It's going to blow!"

Roslyn races for the street. The furnace man yanks her behind his van and they crouch elbow to elbow, as if playing hide and seek. Three. Two. One. They peek. The furnace man makes a call. They stand shoulder to shoulder. A city bus grinds by.

"Guess I capped 'er in time." The man lights a smoke. "Make yourself comfortable. We can't go in until my superior gets here." He squats and takes a drag. "You're damn lucky you had the flood, ma'am. Those pipes are so loose, when I tried to shut off a valve they came apart in my hands. Natural gas pouring out." He shakes his head and does a slow exhale. "Woulda happened at some point. Kaboom! You and your house—" He points skyward. "Headin' for Oz, lady. Be grateful for the goddamn flood."

The phone is ringing when Roslyn re-enters the house.

"Roslyn. I've got it! It's a brimming over of Floyd's desire!

---

8   A special mode where everything on the playfield scores a lot of points.

A bursting-through of repressed hankering between the two of you. You've got to consummate it, Roslyn. You've got to let yourself go!"

Jackpot[9]

Friday, September 2nd. 1:28 p.m. The adjustor phones Roslyn to say her claim has been approved — insurance will pay — new washer, dryer, furnace, water heater, flooring, pipes, stepper, stationary bike. Roslyn puts the phone down in her crimson kitchen. She feels ravenous. Flips on the computer. Looks up her birth year. The Water Dragon. "Water Dragons sit on a pedestal when it comes to love."

2:34 p.m. Kouzie's mother gets a call from Arizona. Ardythe's taken off with Duck's credit card. Will she have him back?

3:18 p.m. Kouzie buzzes his mother down Highway 3 toward the Cranbrook airport. The wind from the west, nuzzling, warm, wild. The sun, a horny spike of fire burning down the sky. The moon has started her silver ascent. Kouzie's mouth waters. At the terminal entrance he kisses his mother's dry cheek. Pulls out his cell. Takes a deep breath. Dials Sylvia's number.

---

9   Scoring in pinball games is a mystery to most amateur players, whose basic goal is simply to keep the ball from going down the drain. The pinball expert, however, is after much more: ultimately, to win the Super Jackpot.

Cool shadows lick, blue-grey and reaching, against Vancouver streets. 4:46 p.m. Stella sits on her tall steps in a gold metallic cocktail dress with a silver sash. Bicyclists zip the summer streets below. Blinky has fled Stella's perfect kitchen for good; Splasho hasn't returned. But, hey, the nail buffer does its job. Stella feels the energy flowing out through her front door, pouring down her steps, carrying her along. The cosmos in motion. Whetting its appetite. Keeping time. Stella closes her eyes against the evening's shimmer. Her body humming.

6:12 p.m. Floyd sails past the foothills on the highway to Calgary, whistling along to the oldie-goldies. "Nights in White Satin." "You Really Got Me." "A Change Is Gonna Come." Tonight he's taking Roslyn out for dinner. To celebrate that insurance will pay. That Roslyn's basement has been licked clean. He knows a good Chinese in the northeast quadrant. Triangular cookies to tell their fortunes. Then he'll drive her to Strathmore's End of Summer Fair. They'll lick soft ice cream, ride the Ferris wheel. Swinging down and around, rocking over the earth. Floyd's body solid in his seat. Roslyn, smelling like summer earth, circling beside him. Floyd preens like a peacock. He speeds through Black Diamond. His ankles disappearing in the darkening dusk. The Ferris wheel will pause atop the cosmos before it oscillates and starts its vibrating descent. Floyd smells summer ending, it rips at his chest as they pitch over the delicious edge, fireworks scattering in the cold night air.

Mr. Bloxham's
Happiness

———————

Duncan Bloxham is drinking, stuffed in his armchair, watching Jadwiga clean the pots. His drinking glass jiggles against his knee. He pours another scotch and draws in a wheeze. It feels years since he's had a wife. He has the niggling feeling he should entertain her, or she'll start dusting, end up on her knees, muttering to her rosary. One thing Duncan can't abide is prayer. The problem is he married a Pole. Turns out she doesn't know her arse from her elbow. Doesn't even keep Keen's Mustard on hand. What kind of person doesn't keep Keen's? He may be living in Canada, but the British do things properly. It's inbred. It's the reason they've always conquered. For instance? Yesterday was Sunday. Did Jadwiga make Sunday roast? Oh, the woman went to church so she knew it was Sunday. She knew. But what did she do to spite him? Served horrid little sausages on kabobs! Then made a dash for her bloody beads, crying, "But they're a national dish!"

"Aren't you something!" Duncan had chuckled. "Go ahead! Have your little opinions!" It didn't matter a fig to him! It didn't matter to him at all! It made no difference! None whatsoever! He fears an inferior intellect. What kind of people think it normal to say, The cat *black* is *in* the table? There's a reason English is the world's international language. What's this? Now the woman's brought him tea. With cream!! He catches her elbow. Enunciates. Let. Me. Explain. This. Once. Again. *Cream* goes in coffee. *Whole milk* goes in tea. He should have stuck with a wife who understood tradition.

Out in the yard the neighbour's dog scrabbles and scratches in the garden, leaking, leaking from his bloody cysts.

Duncan sighs. What's the woman doing now? Bavarding on the telephone in Polish. Most likely complaining to her sister in some old cold city. Sausageville. He wouldn't normally get mixed up with peasants. A lapse of good judgment. Happens to the best man. He can't take her to the public library. No Harlequin Romances there in Polish. They can't go to a coffee shop; Jadwiga's so fat he's got her on carrots and apples and prunes, bird seed, crushed walnuts and pumpkin pits. If the woman sees food, she's wild to eat. She squashes the receiver against her ear with one pudgy hand, trying to climb through the telephone wires. The squiggly material across her backside swishes and sways as she wipes down the cupboards. Christ! She isn't using disinfectant. An utter and total waste of time! Oh, lord, turn on the tears. What are you babbling? I knew it. I knew you'd want to go back. I'll buy the Christly ticket myself! Even a careful man makes mistakes.

§

Jadwiga punches the telephone numbers, emitting short sharp bursts of air, followed by a humming sound. She holds together her wobbling knees. Mr. Bloxham disapproves of widespread thighs. She pictures a shelf of plump tomatoes. "I weel have toooo," she says in English under her breath, in case Mr. Bloxham, waking from a nap, suddenly sends her to a shop. He's been springing orders like a Russian general. Make Yorkshire puddings! Sweep the sidewalk! Peel the mushrooms! Put on Tchaikovsky! Anticipation sets her on edge. Talking to her sister in Vilnius will help. The telephone sounds in Jadwiga's ear, two spiky buzzes, Bssst. Bssst. A starling outside the open window begins a frantic feather-dusting. Starlings in Poland cluster in groups, but Canada is a lonely place. Ahhhhh. Jadwiga allows her knees to sink open an instant, then squeezes them shut. Mr. Bloxham finds her *tłusty, opasły*. He watches women on the television, waists measuring the size of Jadwiga's calf. A Pole wants a woman who can inhale with ease. For this she needs ample buttocks and breasts. Mr. Bloxham has the windows open — "airing" — though it is March and minus sixteen. She risks a glance across the room. There he is, perched in his armchair; ready, set to catapult. Jadwiga doesn't know much about British husbands. She has been married only six days. She clenches, fearing a nervous seepage, and snaps a photo of the refrigerator with her cell phone hidden in her clasped hand, the landline receiver still squashed to her ear. She underhandedly shoots the toaster. Appliances are an even bigger hit with her sister and her ninety-two-year-old mother than landing herself a British husband.

"Where is my mauve Italian shirt?!" Mr. Bloxham, jouncing on the balls of his feet. A trick question on a live game show! Jadwiga is wild for American game shows. But Mr. Bloxham, onto her tricks, switches channels when she darts behind him to watch a wild-haired woman fill in the letters of "for-ni-ca-tion", shriek, jump in the air, and win a car.

"Not a cloo," Jadwiga says. She should have married a North Korean. North Koreans seem a grateful bunch.

"My. Mauve. Shirt." Mr. Bloxham repeats, picking a thread of meat from his teeth. A second chance for half the money! Bssst. Bssst goes the telephone in Bożenna's dingy apartment by the river in Vilnius. Vilnius, no longer a Polish city; it now resides in Lithuania. Jadwiga's sister residing in Vilnius since she studied at the medical school. And here's Jadwiga, with a British husband, residing in icy Canada! The thread of meat hangs from Mr. Bloxham's lip. Mr. Bloxham used the steak and kidney pie (the kidneys smelling of onions and urine), for a demonstration of how to eat "properly" using at once a knife and fork in loo of stabbing peasant-style. Loo means toilet. Why use loo within this sentence? Jadwiga doesn't need a knife and fork, shovelling seeds and nuts and chunks of raw carrot. She expels a quarter cup of breath. A litre sigh puts Mr. Bloxham off. He demands to know what she's sighing for and Jadwiga doesn't have a large imagination.

§

Two weeks with a wife and what does he find? Her morning bowel movement in the refrigerator. Perched above the salad drawer. Still steaming. "Jadwiga! Get yourself in here!" Where has she gone? Is she taking the mick? "Jadwiga!" Into the kitchen she lumbers, trailing her dust rag, sweat shining her forehead. That baggy dress! Do Poles wash in the river? Whack their laundry with rocks?

"What is *this?!*" Duncan dangles between thumb and finger a cloudy Tupperware container. The two stare down at the large beige lump.

"Fee-cee," Jadwiga enunciates. And to Duncan Bloxham's incredulous harrumph, "I heff blood in my stew-all." Jadwiga thumps her large behind in case Duncan might wonder from whence stool emerges. She swipes her forehead with the dusting cloth and she's off to slap at his figurines, leaving Duncan glaring at the scarlet veins rivering the lump like beet juice injections.

"Well, bloody hell, you don't need a kilo!" Duncan slams the lid on, whams shut the fridge door. He pictures Jadwiga without any hair. Will he have to put up with croaky dry heaves? Then go through the whole courting process all over? Three wives have already flown the coop. Lord, is there not one competent woman in the western hemisphere?

Duncan orders Tetley tea. Jadwiga, grunting, bends for the kettle. He listened to some rat-arsed plonker's advice in a bar in Vancouver: *Polish women are eager to please.* He advertised in the *Kraków News,* and caught a flight to observe his prospects. His first interviewee arrived on a bicycle, rucksack sweated to her sticky back. Brilliant colours swirling her ill-fitting clothes as she mouth-breathed up the hotel driveway. A huge bottle of something bobbed on her hip. Purple wires of varicose veins disappeared into her knee-length trousers.

The woman started in interviewing Duncan before he could get his papers shuffled, and everything went to cock from there. Did Canada have public transit? The woman disapproved of public transit. She'd be bringing her forty-two-year old son, and her ancient rusty basketed bicycle — needless to say, she pedaled back home.

Jadwiga slides open the baking drawer, and nabs a handful of chocolate chips. Duncan chooses to ignore it. Triumphant, she turns to her rising rye bread dough. Punching and squinting at the dissonant mound.

Duncan orders another cup of tea. Just to show Jadwiga who's boss. The second woman arrived by taxi. Announced — as if this deserved an award — that she was most attentive to laundry. She would change the beds. But *do cholery!* Every week?! Most certainly not. Weekly washing? A waste of water! Were the British scared off by a bit of dirt?! She peered at Duncan as if at an inferior specimen. She, a Pole! And he a Brit! She was tall, round-shouldered, fifty-seven years old. Everything about the woman sloped. Her knees, her eyelids, her skin-hung elbows. Even her breasts looked down on Duncan. At the end of the day, he chose short, stocky Jadwiga, who bobbed up the driveway on bulgy legs, grinning behind her sweat-stained glasses and proud as punch of her sparkly belt. When Duncan asked from what part of Poland she hailed, Jadwiga waved vaguely in all directions, and said a mouthful that sounded like: Between two rivers and two great forests. Duncan pictured a fairytale.

He chose Jadwiga because his head ached; through the pounding haze she looked pleasingly plump. And she didn't request a heated mattress to massage her aching knees. Didn't demand meals taken undisturbed. She didn't demand her own large-screen telly. She didn't demand anything at all. Duncan found her polka-dot vest endearing. She sweated buckets and kept rubbing her glasses. She said laundry in Canada would be a pleasure with the country's modern machinery. She announced with vehemence that she bathed daily, as if Duncan had suggested she smelled. Thanks-God, she said at the news of the Catholic Church, Our Lady of Perpetual Help, up the street from Duncan's house. That cinched it. A Catholic would never steal. Socks scared off by purgatory.

Well, here she is, all ninety kilos of her, rubbing the gold inlay off his bloody chairs. In Poland she polished stones for a living. Worked for a doctor of research, she said. The morning after their marriage, he let her loose on his French furniture. Red-faced, determined, she scoured pieces down. He must send them out; redo the gilt-edging.

Duncan's tea is cold. He phones the doctor, explains the emergency.

"Blud in da stewall. Blud in da stewall," Jadwiga mutters happily as she gathers her coat and her fuchsia handbag. Duncan waits six minutes while she searches for her belt, then loads his fat and cheerful wife into the automobile — she too owned a bicycle in Poland; a car ride's like being at the county fair. Jadwiga is grinning, black eyes gleaming shards as Duncan slides to a halt at the four-way stop, sunlight glinting off the icy streets. He nearly collides with a yellow school bus that rolls right through; a kid gives him the finger out the back window.

Jadwiga holds the pile of poo on her lap as if it's a gift from God, until Duncan snaps it out of her hand. For the remainder of the ride to the clinic, it ricochets between them on the console, Jadwiga giving it paranoid clobbers as they jostle the icy corners.

Jadwiga starts muttering to her rosary—does the woman think that God speaks Polish?!—one hand clouting the feces bucket, the other squeezing tight her handbag. Her eyelashes are extraordinarily long. Another reason Duncan chose her. He blurted his admiration in a post-orgasm spasm on their wedding night. Jadwiga, huffing, rolled onto her side, as if she were the one who had done the work.

"Glow-co-muhhh."

"I beg your pardon?" Duncan wheezed. Sex is strenuous exercise for a man of his age. He had almost forgotten the bursts of work required when you don't perform alone. He peered through the darkness to make out Jadwiga, evidently playing charades. "Glow-comb-uh!" Hand in the air, finger aimed at her eye, grinning: "Glow-com-a. Side eee-ffect."

Duncan fell back against the mattress. He'd married a woman whose one strong trait—her lovely eyelashes—were the result of *disease!*

What bloody tricksters women are! Duncan steers the car into the clinic car park.

"Pe-can," Jadwiga mutters into her coat collar. "Bran flakes. Cho-co-late. Tap-ee-o-ka."

Is the woman trolleyed? Duncan marches ahead.

§

Rye bread. Pork belly. Roasted garlic. Jadwiga's stomach rumbles as she waits on the waiting room chair. She pictures Mr. Bloxham preparing a feast: pork feet, potatoes, and shredded beets. But this would require Mr. Bloxham to be somebody else entirely. She runs a tube of lotion around her ears. The air in Canada frightfully dry.

The night they married, on his best behavior, Mr. Bloxham asked, "How does one say 'have sex' in Polish?" Wherever would Jadwiga begin? There is a Polish expression for "copulation." There is a Polish expression for "intercourse." Each pair of lovers creates their own language. Would never share those words with another. Jadwiga, straight-backed beside Mr. Bloxham, buffing his nails on the waiting-room chair — Mr. Bloxham suffers from vanity — thinks of Aloizy, her late husband. Across the room, a woman is knitting something large and lime-green. Aloizy kissed her hand after every dance. How to explain such love to Mr. Bloxham? Jadwiga imagines Mr. Bloxham dancing. In her mind he dances irritably. Mr. Bloxham bought her a Polish–English–English–Polish dictionary for a wedding present — it is very large — and a bar of soap, as if encouraging her to wash. The dictionary has a section named "Slang." After considerable consultation, Mr. Bloxham laid the book on the bedside chair, and said politely in very bad Polish: "Lie down and spread them." Jadwiga did. Her new husband thinks she's a *kurcze*. Jadwiga sighs, squeezes the container.

"What's wrong?" Mr. Bloxham snaps, dropping his nail buffer into his pocket. Sighing in Canada is disallowed.

The problem is Aloizy's dead. Sailed right off the earth, and now she's here in this foreign country that smells of lettuce and is blue with cold. She attempts, under Mr. Bloxham's stare, to button Aloizy into a body bag so she can stop mourning, be a wife to this husband, but Aloizy's eyes and nose and a flap of wavy hair stick out when she tries to stuff him in. Dead almost two years. Jadwiga believed she too would die of a heart condition, left on earth while Aloizy's ghost mournfully moon-walked her darkened rooms.

"You must leave the country. He will stay in Poland," her mother and sister, so bossy, promised, but Aloizy rode baggage to Canada.

A woman enters with a little square girl resembling a stump. Jadwiga sucks back air so she doesn't sigh at the sight of the child, who closes her eyes and begins a dance, as if shot repeatedly with a stun gun. Aloizy, a sweet and handsome labourer from the neighbouring village came to work for her father, and she was smitten. When the boys in her village got the news that Jadwiga — whose dark beauty turned men into animals — and Aloizy were about to marry, they beat Aloizy. They broke his knees. Work was difficult after but he never complained. With Aloizy, Jadwiga savoured lovemaking. She stifles a hiccup, shoots a glance at this husband. The problem: she doesn't burn for Mr. Bloxham. To make up for her terrible shortcoming, she cleans and cleans. Yesterday she found a pan in the cupboard, black as soot. It said *Teflon* on it. All day she scrubbed at the blackened coating, at last scraping down to the silver beneath. Whatever had Mr. Bloxham burned within it?!

The child slouches back into her seat, her long feet sticking out in bright red trainers. Jadwiga grew up with fourteen siblings. Her parents had a hut, a garden, a goat. She got her first pair of shoes when the Soviets came. Now at sixty-two she's landed a foreigner. This country isn't his country either. But Mr. Bloxham acts like it is.

§

A gentleman would hold a lady's feces, but Duncan Bloxham has his limits. The dreadful child stares at the container. Duncan snatches it from Jadwiga's fingers and shoves it underneath his chair.

Three parents. Two newborns. A preschool boy. And the too-short gyrating girl who drops crinkled worksheets in a messy pile and plays with the shoehorn she extracts from her mother's handbag. The baby squalls. Its mother keeps giving in to spit-stringed yawns. "Eight days," she tells the huge woman with long yellow-grey hair, jabbing a thumb at her crying baby. "A breach."

"They're all trouble," the fat woman says, "Aren't they, Daddy?" she elbows her little husband, crammed in beside her.

Duncan's heel smacks the container.

"Oh, careful, da stew-all!" Jadwiga beams around the waiting room. Duncan shuts her down with a protracted stare.

"Two babies to cheer us!" the fat woman says, gesturing at the wizened newborns. The first baby rages at this news, hard fists pummelling the air like two miniature peppers.

"This is going to be a good day, Daddy."

"Is the doctor a lady?" Daddy cracks his knuckles.

The woman scratches the top of her head, hard and fast, with all four fingers and thumb. "Women are better at doctoring. *We* had a daughter," she tells the exhausted mother.

"She ran away," her husband says.

"Our cat did!" the preschool boy says, delighted.

"Do you know, Daddy," she grabs the man's arm, "that this very minute, the doctors studying in the United States are fifty-seven per cent female?"

"Well that's only half," her husband says.

"*More* than half!"

"*A bit* more than half."

"Mrs. Bloxham?"

Duncan rises, and Jadwiga trails him into a white room with paper towelling on a high narrow cot. The preschool boy races after them, hands squeezed around the Tupperware container. "Ma says don't forgot your poo."

§

Jadwiga lies on the enormous paper towel, closes her eyes, suspends her breathing. How else to know if Mr. Bloxham loves her? She loosens her sparkly belt, peeps through her quivering eyelashes.

Mr. Bloxham hasn't disappeared.

§

Duncan Bloxham is drinking, stuffed in his armchair, watching Jadwiga scour the kettle. All his nerve endings exposed. Well, we shall see who is going to win! He pours another scotch and draws in a wheeze. His thumbnail has turned black for no good reason. The air filling the house has become hard to breathe. A terrible ache stretches down his left leg. This morning a bird hit the window and dropped dead beneath it. This foreign woman, she's smart as a whip. A woman who knows her arse from her elbow. The doctor has just telephoned. The blood in the stool isn't human blood. It's blood alright. The blood of a chicken.

Duncan Bloxham swallows a gulp of whisky.

§

Jadwiga presses flat palms against her stomach, soft like bread dough under her nightdress. She mutters her rosary in her head, steps into her childhood sweet shop, a little closet smelling of ginger and raspberries. Picks up *kröwki,* a soft brown square, wrapped like candy inside a picture of a yellow cow. The short bald shopkeeper holds her gaze, hands the package across the counter.

"Pancake," she whispers, "Shoo-horn. Per-foom."

Mr. Bloxham's mournful whistle circles their dark cold bed.

A Lovely Hind,
A Graceful Doe

The deer leaps over the embankment. Crashes against Roslyn's seven-year-old Toyota Tercel with a dreadful thunk, one deer head, one wild eye rammed up her windshield, Roslyn mid-sing-along to Jann Arden's "Good Mother." Mother FU—! The stunned deer, after his startling cameo — mouth mashed ajar as if warbling harmony — keeps right on hustling, galumphing down the ditch on its broken legs. Roslyn, hiccupping hysterically, steers the car — squealing, hissing, sending out its own agitated symbols of distress — to a stop on the side of the Crowsnest Highway, the injured creature stumbling and reeling toward the bush in her rear-view mirror, Jann Arden calling after it how her heart is in her hands — Arden can't know the first thing about it. Roslyn violently snaps off the radio, leans out the car door. Gags.

When she can sit up, she paws for her purse, blows her nose in one of her pilfered stash of Duncan's monogrammed DB handkerchiefs, made in the UK, and gapes at herself in the mirror. Her eyes stare back like two raw eggs. She grips the wheel, heart beating against her stomach lining; head a whistling void.

After some time, Roslyn pulls shakily back onto the highway, eyes flitting the ditches. She can snivel all she wants, but she has a wedding to get to that starts in eighteen minutes. Now and then her bumper clunks the highway, cascading a trail of sparks. Every couple of metres the tailpipe backfires. But, by some miracle, the car still runs. Roslyn tramps her brand new green satin Mother-of-the-Groom high-heeled shoe onto the accelerator and rattles past a rumbling RV, grimly steered by an ill-tempered senior; in the passenger's seat, her bebopping husband, wearing an expression of demented merriment, piano-chording up and down the dash.

Roslyn had every intention of leaving Calgary early yesterday morning for the drive to Theo's wedding in Fernie, BC. Help with last-minute decorating. Show Andrea, who she doesn't even know, what kind of great mother-in-law she'll be. But in the last three days Roslyn's bathroom sink plugged (the plumber said it would cost one hundred and twenty dollars just to set foot in her front door), her dishwasher started spewing smoke on the rinse cycle, and she got another threatening letter from Revenue Canada. Early Thursday morning she was awakened by a racket — some guy breaking into her back yard shed. Roslyn sprang out the door in her housecoat and slippers, scaring the bejesus out of the fellow who took off down the back alley, clattering her lawn mower across the gravel at impressive speed until her twenty-five foot cord caught under the sharp tin of the sliding door. Knocked the guy flat. He staggered up, slapping gravel off the back of his head, and limped off, threatening to sue. That afternoon, the brakes in her car started squealing. Didn't Harold always lecture: squealing brakes plus mountains = death sentence? All this in the midst of prepping for her fall classes and picking other people's dog crap off her lawn, to say nothing of trying to unplug the sink herself with a giant knitting needle, grey soap-scum shooting everywhere. She couldn't get the car dropped off at the garage until after the place had closed Thursday evening. In her distress, she shoved her house key, along with her car key, through the little round hole cut in her mechanic's steel garage door. There she was, twisting and stretching, ear squashed against cold steel, trying to wrench the key back out. Nearly wedged herself in for the night. Arm scraped and stinging, she had to walk home through the industrial part of town in the dark, past snarling German shepherds and Rottweilers barely penned in by chain-link · fences topped with barbed wire. Exhausted, she climbed into bed for another near-sleepless night, staring down the dark-ness, reviewing her snag lists: 1. All the Ways She's Let Theo Down; 2. All the Ways She'll Make it up to Him, starting with her knock-out designer Mother-of-the-Groom dress. Single shoulder strap. Tear-drop peek-a-boo back. Studded sliver of a black belt. Probably diamonds, considering the price tag. A dress to say to Theo, Nothing's too good for you. Won't hurt either to show Harold's wife — to say noth-ing of Harold — that she's still got it, and she can flaunt it. The garage didn't finish her tune-up until nine-thirty this morning. By the time she raced to get the car, wrestled her suitcase down her steep front stairs, and jumped behind the wheel in her shiny green show-stopper dress, her armpits were soaked — oh god, let the deer be dead.

When she finally fell asleep last night, what did she dream? Shit. Poopy overflowing toilets. A manure spreader sending dung clots whizzing over a rhubarb patch. A soccer field of shit that she and Theo sat in, side by side, legs straight out, cheerfully doing calisthenics.

And now she's hit a deer.

A singular pinpoint pokes Roslyn's chest from the inside as if she is about to choke on one popcorn kernel. A gopher darts across the highway. She hits the brakes, tires squealing, heart rat-a-tatting. *Get a grip!* Reminds Roslyn of the time she and Harold drove to northern Alberta to visit the relatives. It was early on in their marriage. They still shared a favourite song: "Video Killed the Radio Star." Theo was still in his car seat, just starting to talk. They passed a marsh and Harold slammed on the brakes as birds flew low across the road. All three of them lurched against their seatbelts. Theo mistook this for some awesome game Harold had created solely for Theo's riding pleasure. "Oh, wow!" he hollered from the back seat in his high, strident voice. "Daddy. More! Oh wow!" Then worked himself into a screaming tantrum when Harold wouldn't produce. They stumbled out of the van at Harold's parents' house in Hinton forty minutes later, ears ringing, to discover a Canada goose, sprawled against the radiator in a centrefold spread, wingtip to wingtip, beak mashed into the grill. An awe-struck Theo, faith in his father restored, looked on while Harold and his dad pried the bird off, feathers floating into gardens like the dislodged wings of some dysfunctional angel, neighbours snapping photos. The goose,

Theo — mouth circled around a wide-vowelled Wow! — and their dented van all made the front page of the *Hinton Voice*.

Theo used to get laryngitis, he talked so much. "Remember the time we camped above the railroad yard in the fog and Daddy dropped his hammer over the cliff. . ." Theo, cut-and-pasting himself into stories. He wasn't even born when Harold nearly doinged the railway worker. Well, Roslyn can't imagine all the stories Theo's now front and centre in that she isn't privy to. Is Harold? Is *Evelyn?* She glances in the rear-view mirror at her mascara, clumped and smudged. Brushes an eyelash off her cheek. She considered asking Stella to be her date. Someone to talk to in those moments everyone else will be standing around in chummy little circles. But Stella has a new guy, fresh out of AA, who rides a scooter to his anger management and watercolour classes. Admit it, Roslyn: she thought of asking Floyd. But how could she, after the way she'd left things; it wouldn't have been fair. How lovely though, to have had Floyd walk her through this day. Floyd, with his naked Doukhobor stories, his sweet way of calling her Good-Lookin', of saying, Don't worry your pretty little head. Floyd, rebuilding the shambles of her house after her divorce from Duncan. If she and Floyd — Jesus, Roslyn! They haven't spoken since he drove the last nail in her reno fifteen months ago. Since she drove the final nail in the coffin of whatever-it-was-they'd-had. "Calgary. Y. Yorkton," Roslyn says aloud, playing the game she conjured to distract Theo on car trips. The man probably doesn't even own a suit. "N. Nelson. N. Nebraska. A. Amsterdam. M. Medicine Hat . . ."

Just let the goddamn deer be dead.

Roslyn skids to a stop in front of the clubhouse, eight minutes late, her car a raucous bluegrass band of banjo plinks and clacking spoons. She tosses her keys to the open-mouthed valet, and takes off sprinting in her green high heels for the outdoor wedding behind the golf course clubhouse. The clear summer sky has morphed into a spill of ominous, hurtling clouds. Well, when has the September long weekend not signalled the beginning of the end?

Roslyn rounds the corner onto the flower-laden green. She can see the back of Harold's wife's violently back-combed hair in the front row. No time to find a washroom —she is set upon by a gap-toothed red-headed usher, whose apparent orders have been: Stand By to Nab the Mother-of-the-Groom! He bounces to her side—somebody's glad she's here — grandly offers his arm, and before she has time to check her teeth, Roslyn is being trotted up the aisle. Theo's mother, fashion chic at 9 a.m., but here at 2:11, a wrinkled-silk-organza wreck with dry-stained armpits, her elbows snapped tight against her sides to hide the water rings, probably cutting off the circulation in this poor boy's hand. She should have got a prescription for Ativan.

She also should have checked those Spanx advertisements. She's gained six pounds in the last six months — all those Chocolate Eruptions at The Main Dish when she was feeling down. But hey! Roslyn straightens her shoulders, tilts her chin — hasn't she bought a year's gym pass? Isn't she working her inner thighs? Roslyn imagines herself in a Doris Day musical, bursting into song. "My Dreams Are Getting Better All the Time."

Theo stands on the grass, hands clasped before him, facing the open-air canopy and the rows of guests beneath it on their folding chairs. Her Theo. In a tux. The usher glances at her in alarm. Theo's haircut — same bristly trim that graced his head in elementary school. Shoes so shiny she goes temporarily blind.

To the left of the bridesmaid stands a young man in a shiny-kneed suit, eyes darting the crowd like a bodyguard's. Now and then he hauls in a breath. Andrea's minister was hospitalized Wednesday with a massive heart attack. Roslyn learned this when she telephoned Theo to say she'd be a day late. The youth minister will be the stand-in. Theo grants Roslyn a wary, fleeting smile as she takes the aisle seat beside Harold in the front row.

And here they are. Roslyn and Evelyn, wives past and present, Harold pressed between them like a large damp book.

"Where the hell have you been?!" Harold whispers.

Balls smack, somewhere across the green. They knock inside Roslyn's head. She yanks at the skirt of her dress. "I hit a deer!" A splat of rain splashes off her shoe.

"A what? She *hit a what?*" the woman on Evelyn's far side whispers, jerking forward to stare at Roslyn. One dangly earring, bent at its joint, sticks out at a crazy angle, aimed at Roslyn's head like a stun dart.

"My mother-in-law," Harold says, then, in a loud strained whisper, "A *deer!*"

They all three sigh — Harold, Evelyn, her mother — saddened that Harold's ex mows down wild animals on her way to weddings. What is *Evelyn's* mother doing here? She's not even related! Seated beside the mother-in-law, a woman of similar age stares at her ankles, muttering, "Dear, dear," fist against her chest, as if her thoughts are stirring heartburn.

"Evelyn's aunt," Harold whispers. Leans closer, "Dementia."

Splat! Splat-Splat-Splat! The light pattering on the giant tarp augments to a drumming deluge. Theo, the best man, and the electric-purple bridesmaid take one look at each other and make a dash for it. The young minister, after a moment's hesitation, lopes after them. They press in among the guests crowding toward the canopy's centre to avoid the slanting rain slashing in the open sides, everyone talking at once over the din, stumbling against chairs, nose-diving into each others' arms, shrieking with laughter. It's as if Roslyn missed the wedding after all and has been beamed straight to the reception. Blasts of deodorant, dampened hairspray, a shot of Avocado-and-Vanilla-Mint-Essential-Blend. Bushes bent horizontal on the golf course. The minister stares mournfully at his sermon papers, lifting, sailing above the canopy like doves, disintegrating into wet bits, plummeting, sagging against the grass. He takes a dejected step back. Treads on Harold's foot. "I'm so sorry!" Harold whacks him on the back. "Apology accepted!" Pumping, pumping the man's hand, as if a foot-stamp wins the young man some kind of prize. "My wife!" Harold beams, draping an arm over Evelyn's broad cerise-poplinned shoulders. "Oh, and my ex-wife, Roslyn," as if she isn't even Theo's mother. The minister exclaims, "Ex-wife!" and shoots a terrified, jellified smile, like a man with a shotgun in his face. "I didn't used to be this short!" he says into the burst of silence.

Everybody laughs too hard. Then Harold and Evelyn and her mother sidestep off in the opposite direction and talk amongst themselves. Roslyn and the demented aunt leave the muttering minister, wander back to their seats, and set about examining their knees for scaly patches.

The marriage will end. Of course it will end. Harold's grandma died on Roslyn and Harold's wedding day, fifteen miles from the church, Saskatchewan gravel road, massive heart attack, 1:22 p.m. Thirty-eight minutes before Roslyn walked up the aisle to crazy glue herself to Harold. And look what happened to *their* marriage.

"Dear, dear," the demented aunt moans, four chairs down, as if reading Roslyn's thoughts.

Harold's other grandma — the miserable one, Harold's mother's mother, who called the police on three occasions to report that her daughter was stealing 1. her photo albums; 2. her brassieres; 3. her dessert spoons — lived fifteen more rage-soaked years.

Roslyn. Mother-of-the-Groom. Harbinger of bad luck.

What *is* it lately with animals? A hare has taken up residence under the chaise longue in her back yard. Her neighbour caught sight of a little red fox trotting down the walkway along the side of her house early one morning. And a coyote has started stalking her on the running trail, skimming along with his dog-track swivel, as if they're out for their morning jaunt. One day, Roslyn, jogging up the path behind the Kensington Safeway with a package of honey-garlic chicken wings, was forced to turn and take repeated shrieking lunges (great for cardio) just to scare the brazen creature a few feet back, till she made the top of the hill and the safe collection of houses. A ploy honed in the final throes of her marriage to Duncan.

The sluicing rain diminishes to a series of spits, and drifts away on swollen lavender clouds. Everyone retakes their places.

The young minister raises his arms. "Honoured guests. Please rise for the entry of the bride!"

Andrea.

She stands at the path's head, her silky red hair tumbling over bony shoulders jagging out of sockets of lace. Harold mouth-breathes on Roslyn's neck, craning to see.

"*Veg*etables?!" he says.

Vegetables. The bride thrusts before her a bouquet of vegetables. Large vegetables. Artichoke, red and orange bell peppers on some sort of stick, broccoli, an eggplant, several leeks, peeled purple onions, heads of garlic poking through, garnished with parsley, cilantro, sage, and mint. She smells like a cooking class. The violinist on a knoll to their right, in a Swiss vest and a fedora, starts a brisk sawing on his instrument. The wind hauls the notes off in the opposite direction across the green, flings them at a far line of trees. The musician, unaware, mimes on.

The bride steps forward. Ta-daa! A hyperventilating dog pops from behind her skirts. Wanda! Her sparkling mauve leash attached somewhere within Andrea's perky vegetables.

Andrea gives the leash a little tug. And they're off. For a brief moment the sun, hanging in the moist air like a mushy brown peach, lights the bride's head, a quick explosion, and she turns into a thin lit match burning up the aisle. Fifth row in, Wanda drops onto her butt, front paws waving, and scoots along the wet grass past the next four rows in an extended anus-itch. The crowd breaks up. The minister develops a face rash. Andrea good-humouredly skids Wanda along. Her eyes latch onto Theo's. Grins pivot between them.

Anxiety pummels Roslyn's chest. How will they live? Theo still hasn't organized himself to go back to school. He works in restaurants till he has enough money for his next adventure. He can barely afford his rent. Margaret's voice clips into Roslyn's head: "September second? Roslyn, we can't! The Dominican Republic. It's been booked for months! No, we can't change it! Well, you'd have expected him to check with his own aunt! Though what am I saying?" Across the phone lines Roslyn could see her sister's lips pinch in reprimand. "The boy's own mother didn't invite her son *or* sister to *her* wedding. Why in heaven's name is he getting married so fast? He hasn't got her pregnant?" Roslyn peers around the bouquet of vegetables, while Evelyn's aunt slides forward on her chair, nylons rasping, and peers behind her to the outdoor patio where the reception bar is set up, as if she can't wait to drink.

Evelyn grabs Harold's meaty hand, pressing white spots beneath his knuckles. "Oh, sweetie, isn't she a dream!" Harold's wife, believer in Happily Ever After. Evelyn, whose last husband left her with two babies under two the day the moving truck delivered their belongings to their new house in the burbs. "The asshole never showed." Harold related this story when he and Roslyn met at The Purple Perk to discuss the wedding, who'd pay for what. Harold came with two completed lists. His. Hers. Ordered two rhubarb crisps. Ate them both. Confided he's taken over writing nasty letters to Evelyn's ex under Evelyn's name. The guy still owes her for the car. Harold's begun to suspect recently that the ex's new wife has taken over writing back under her husband's name. The tone is wittier, Harold said, sharper. Gloves off! Harold waved rhubarb crisp from the end of his fork. Bits of brown sugar crumbs sprinkled the floor beneath them. Evelyn isn't coping well with the stress, Harold admitted, but he'll be damned if he'll quit now. Harold's been married going on two years. Did he have any idea what he was getting into? Was he any better prepared than Roslyn found herself with Duncan?

Duncan. Methodically working his way through her house, room by room, square metre by square metre, scrubbing down all surfaces vertical, horizontal, triangular, and spherical with Shark, Dirt Devil, Quicky MFG, UGG, Mrs. Meyer's Lavender Toilet Cleaner, Mrs. Meyer's Day Spring Clean-Up Kit, Snap Pea Scent, sorting her drawers and cupboards, making heaps of trash on her kitchen floor: the red-glazed lopsided pottery thrown by Margaret (okay, the pieces were ugly, but still), her cayenne, chili, turmeric and curry powders (well, he *did* suffer from gastro-esophageal reflux), her freezer-burned pork chops, the stuffed guinea fowl Uncle Morley sent from Botswana. "How can you live in this crap?" Duncan flung out these items, along with all photos of Roslyn and a man. Any man. Even Theo. She came to picture Duncan as an appliance of some sort, a self-cleaning oven, locked and whirring, burning off the sludge.

The bride and Wanda arrive. Andrea unhands her vegetables, then a panting Wanda, over to the bridesmaid, who Roslyn sees now is an older version of Andrea. Same high cheekbones. Same narrow lips, the bridesmaid's disappearing as she gingerly accepts Wanda's leash and the odorous bouquet. The minister looks on, sucking his lip.

Theo crouches, gives Wanda's head an affectionate gooddog ruffle. Drops her a doggie biscuit that emerges, crumbs included, from his tux pocket while the minister agitatedly yanks off a scrap of paper sticking to his shoe, smoothes it against the music stand, and attempts a frantic silent read. Theo takes Andrea's hands. Squeezes. She squeezes back. The mime packs away his violin. Wanda sniffs each member of the wedding party, pronounces them agreeable, flops on her side, *Whew! Done!* She snuggles down to sun herself. Eyes droop. Her body jerks. The young minister lifts one shoe over Wanda, then withdraws it and walks around her. He straightens his thin shoulders. Draws a huge breath.

"Dearly beloved." Silence. "Here we are." A few titters from beneath the canopy. The minister smiles anxiously. "We are — uh — gathered this afternoon in the presence of — uh — God, and of this congregation, to show our support for Theodore and Angela —"

"Andrea," Theo says.

The young man coughs. "Sorry. Of course. Sorry. Andrea."

He pauses.

"This afternoon is special. For as God tells us in the book of Proverbs, A good woman is hard to find. And when a young man and young woman such as you, Theodore and Angela —"

"Andrea!" says Andrea sharply.

Wanda harrumphs.

The minister flushes deeply up the neck. He closes his

eyes. Perhaps praying for divine intervention or to be beamed straight up to heaven.

He opens them, grips the music stand, smiles. Starts again. "In the sacrament of marriage, God is the zip and you" — he gestures to Theo and Andrea — "are the zipper!" He looks startled, pleased.

Theo and Andrea lean forward, nodding encouragingly.

"A bride — a bride and a groom cannot be one in holy matrimony, without God to join them. And what God zips together man and woman must not — unzip. For in doing so, they break — the zipper, and the article of clothing can — cannot hold itself together. It becomes — divorced. And God *abhors* divorce. He warns —"

Evelyn lunges for Harold's hand. Roslyn glances across the aisle, where Andrea's father is gloomily fondling his new wife, back pointedly turned on Andrea's mother, who has squished herself possessively against her boyfriend, showily running her fingers along his shirt sleeve.

"— embark on this new facet of your life, Theo, be faithful to Angela, and Angela alone." A ripple of laughter. The man looks momentarily stricken. Speeds up. "For richer or for poorer!"

The demented aunt presses both hands to her spleen.

"In sickness or in heal —!"

A vomiting sound. Roslyn looks up — S L O S H! A surging waterfall sluicing, drenching, smacking, plastering her hair against her face, head, dress, underwear soaking. She staggers to her feet — Harold, Evelyn, Evelyn's mother, the aunt staring: aghast, *enthralled* at rivers of water cascading from Roslyn's hem, neckline, armpits. In skids the photographer, snapping, snapping photos of the Mother-of-the-Groom: Roslyn gasping, Roslyn blowing, dripping, spitting, snorting water out her nose. Harold, hopping back and forth, shaking one soaked leg, drawn out heeee-heeeeee-heeees! Theo, mouth one round polka-dotted O.

The demented aunt springs forward, snatches Harold's suit jacket from the back of his chair, flings it over Roslyn's head. Scrubs vigorously. Dousing flames. Andrea's blue eyes, pupils large, peer beneath its folds, she lifts the jacket, brushing Roslyn's sopping hair out of her eyes, is pinning it back — with what? — with the beautiful pearled barrette that a moment ago adorned her own red hair: "Oh Andrea, not — I couldn't —"

"Mrs. —"

"Roslyn," Roslyn puffs.

The sweetest gap-toothed smile. "Okay. Roslyn then." Click. "There."

A drop splots off Roslyn's ear. Andrea's hand lifts to her mouth, eyes shiny, alive. "Theo. Have you got a handker—?" Theo intent on unearthing from the pocket of his tuxedo, like magic, one of Duncan's handkerchiefs — stuck with doggie biscuit bits and dog hair. Theo intent on handing it over. Andrea intent on passing it on. She and Theo look past each other. Roslyn takes it, mops the rivulets trickling her neck. The minister scurries past, dipping to squeeze at his splashed socks. "I'm so awfully sorry!" Harold galumphing after him, guffawing, holding a sock and a shoe. A hoot explodes from Theo. Andrea falls against him, overcome with the shakes. They wheeze in silent laughter, Wanda, leaping, flinging herself at them, until, in a riot of joyous energy, she tears lickety-split, three times around the tent's perimeter. People crowd, pointing out the edge of the canopy of canvas roof that stretched, dipped in the rainstorm to form a basin. Filled itself with rain. Enough to collect an impressive pool. Timed, aimed, just so.

Evelyn appears beside her. "Oh, you poor, poor thing!" A kind shoulder-squeeze, a sudden reach — Roslyn no time to back away — Evelyn grabbing the skirt of Roslyn's Louis Vuitton eight-hundred dollar Mother-of-the-Groom *statement* with hands adorned by five glittering sharp-crystalled rings, and wringing, wringing, wringing.

"She needs a drink!"

"Get the groom's mom a drink!"

"Will someone just marry them already?!"

"Theo!" Andrea's back, arm encircling Roslyn's shoulder. "We can't! We have to give your mom a chance to dry o —"

Roslyn, Theo's white handkerchief still in hand, signals weakly: No. For christ's sake, get this over. Theo gives her a quick clap on the back and sends Andrea a megawatt grin.

One lone firework shoots off in Roslyn's chest.

The minister places a slim hand on each shoulder. "Repeat after me. I, Angela —" The audience sends up a raucous cheer. Two minutes more and Roslyn's son is a married man. The minister, citing an urgent commitment, escapes down the road.

Roslyn staggers into the bathroom line up, a drip-drying wrinkled walking *derangement*, her dress irrevocably snagged in eleven places by Evelyn's flashing rings. The bridesmaid nips a drink from a bottle in her purse, her monstrously-high electric-purple heels slung over one shoulder. She weaves around to face the demented aunt, "You think I care what people think? I'm going to damn well take my fun when I can get it. I got a kid, remember?! You *seen* Lishia? Well, there you go!"

"O-*kay!*" the old aunt says. She leans in, grabs Roslyn's hand. "Try a hip replacement! See if you care then!" She turns away, twists back, gives Roslyn a disappointed stare. "Oh, if you haven't gone and soaked your head!" She tut-tuts, gestures at the hand-dryer. "Well, go on! *Go* on! Off you go!" Roslyn dutifully sticks her head beneath its roaring.

A crowd of pre-teen boys runs by the open bathroom door, a little ringletted girl in black patents dashes behind, giving everyone the finger.

"Lishia! Come here this instant!" the bridesmaid hollers. The little girl scoots by.

§

Evelyn's mother leans across Roslyn's dessert plate, tops up Roslyn's wine glass, and pours herself another. The speeches are over. The DJ is setting up. Roslyn is still trying to make out what the meat was. It had a wild tang. Evelyn's mother raises her glass, clinks it against Roslyn's. "Evelyn's last husband was a *dick*." She drinks. Touches Roslyn's hand. "A lovely bracelet. I'm having one of my jewellery parties next month. May I send you an invitation?"

The aunt, fork halfway to her mouth, goes rigid. "Where's Roy?"

"Doris. Roy's dead," Evelyn's mother says.

The aunt grabs hold of the table edge, her mouth cracks open, and she cries, hard and silent for a minute, before moving her fork into her mouth for a dainty bite of New York cheesecake.

Evelyn's mother lowers her voice, "Roy died—when did we lose him? Must be 1965."

The aunt shoots Evelyn a terrific glare. "We did *not* lose Roy!" She leans coyly against Roslyn. "I know *exactly* where he is!" She withdraws eight refrigerator magnets from her sweater pockets, and begins ordering the lot.

"Isn't she a case," Evelyn's mother murmurs.

In the kitchen doorway, an inebriated Evelyn, rife with good will, wrestles down a gargantuan garbage bag to the checkered floor.

Hours later, only young ones left on the outdoor dancefloor, the party has degenerated into an uncoordinated, drunken "YMCA." It's chilly out here under the stars next to the canopy, but Roslyn stays. The day has left her with a feeling that is hard to name, as if her chest cavity has split open, and the Milky Way is rushing in.

Harold drifted by some time ago, steering Evelyn to bed. Evelyn's mother, dragging by one arm a battling Lishia, her crying having waned to a low-grade squall, shoes mired in something crusty. "Must be somebody left to hand her over to!" Evelyn's mother saying. The aunt scuttles behind.

Andrea and Theo, slow-dancing, make a turn past Roslyn. A short while ago, an uncle of Andrea's fell to the floor, his wife crying, "Give him air! It's a seizure! Give Herbie air!" Their daughter arguing, "Jeez, Mom. You know what happens when Dad mixes pot with rye." Someone took his arms, another his feet, and they shook him until he came to and stumbled, grinning, back onto the dancefloor.

The bridesmaid, *sans* shoes, has sailed into the night with the photographer.

Roslyn looks out over the darkened golf course, the trembling bushes. The clarity of night air after rain.

"Mom? How you doing?" Theo smells of beer and shampoo, pistachios. "Let's dance."

Roslyn steps into her son's arms.

They circle the empty dancefloor, most of the kids now out behind the building doing something that involves a cheer. Andrea gathers empty beer cans off the pushed-back tables.

Roslyn reaches for the pearl barrette in her frizzled hair; Theo pulls down her hand. "She wants you to keep it."

The night sky falling blue. A draft behind her eyes. "But it's the bride who's supposed to have something borro —"

"You noticed, Mom? Andrea's not one for tradition."

Her son is chatting with her, hand warm on her back.

"Andrea will have her mechanic's license by November." Theo kicks at a crumpled napkin rolling by. "She's thinking of going into business with her brother-in-law. Pete. The guy, balding, who told the kiss-my-ass joke? He owns The Oil Drop."

The wind lifts the canopy roof, ruffles their clothes. Roslyn moves in her son's embrace. Hope, like a planet, circling into view.

She holds it inside her — barely.

They swing past Andrea, laughing with the bartender, leaning against a doorframe, her electric-red hair drooping out of its curls. She signals, two fingers, and Theo gives her a thumbs up.

"Where's Wanda?" The words scrape her throat.

"Sleeping. In our room. She's wiped. Dad and Evelyn'll take her tomorrow."

He's guiding her already to the row of empty chairs. "Okay, Mom. We're go —"

"Theo." Her chest shredding like old wallpaper, in ugly rips. "I hit a deer."

Theo slips onto the chair beside her. "I know. Dad said."

A cheer goes up in the parking lot.

"I didn't mean — I never wanted —"

Her son, twenty-six, stepping away from her. This sudden unnerving inkling that what happened in her life, and what she believed was happening might be two different things. The knowledge rattles through her. "Theo, I wish I'd nev —"

"Mom." Theo's voice is gentle. "Let it go." The night wide open. "Shall we walk you to your room?"

"I'll just sit here a while."

Theo and Andrea gather her bouquet, her veil, her shoes, some cards, a bottle of wine, and disappear into the night.

The DJ packs away his equipment. The bartender closes up. 3:22 a.m. The stars glitter, holes punched in the sky. "We didn't know anything," she says to the DJ, who wheels his giant speakers past her toward the parking lot.

A wind sweeps the golf course, shifting the heavens. The

parking lot erupts in cheers. Roslyn leans her head against the chair. Breathes in. The pain is clean.

The night breeze stirs. The shimmer of an animal, elegant and wild, in the shadowed thicket across the green.

High above, the sky is a riot of sparkling quartz. One star breaks away, skims down the heavens.

Roslyn blinks. There you are.

On Tilt

The Girls

Floyd wriggles the silver tin from his back hip pocket and snaps off the lid. The back door slams, and his granddaughters, pasty from life indoors, hurtle across the lawn, doing the barnyard polka. A sweet ache opens in Floyd watching them shriek as they squish up bits of deer poop with their toes, and he scrapes out a wad of chewing tobacco and stuffs it between his cheek and molars. The girls skid by stiff-legged, bare toes cramped, hooting.

Skoal? That's *women's* chewing tobacco, Kouzie scoffs whenever he drops by to roll a cigarette and wag the jaw. Floyd's no cowboy. He prefers his chewing tobacco mellow. Slipping a wad of Skoal inside his cheek feels like the edge of some memory he can't quite lick onto his tongue. The wood scent of his father's workshop. His father shaking his head saying, Floyd, Floyd, Floyd in his thick Czech accent. Those Fizzies Floyd used to buy after school when he was a kid in Blairmore and had saved ten cents. Agitation. *Something's going to happen.* Sitting at the craps table and you've just rolled a six. Like Floyd feels staring at his kitchen — where to start? Feels like when he used to hold Trevor, fragile as papier mâché. He buys any flavour Skoal comes out with. Cherry. Berry. Peppermint. Takes what's on sale.

Floyd grinds the lawn tractor into gear, flutters his lips like a horse, sits back and he's rolling. He sucks in peppermint, tinged with brandy — adds a few drops so the wad won't dry, so he can swallow instead of spit. He admires his bobbing flowers as he jounces past on the hard metal seat. Roses. Zinnias. Nasturtium. Irises. Every goddamn one made of silk. Deer aren't fond of silk. Blooms never wither. Only time he had a problem was when it rained eight days straight and the sunflower heads plopped off. Waterlogged glue.

"Fifty cents!" Amelia hollers. Legs scissoring, she pumps her fists in the air. Carolyn sprints for her own galvanized pail, white with bird shit, makes her deposit and shouts, "Seventy-five!" Floyd waves at his grandgirls — at this rate they'll have a goodly portion of the deer shit off the lawn by sundown. Call it a game. Throw in a little financial impetus. He gets his yard work done. Everybody's happy. Floyd scratches the girls' numbers on his piece of paper propped against the steering wheel with a pen that has a personality like Trevor's. Only works when it wants.

Trevor

Floyd bounces past the deck where Trevor sprawls, eyes scrunched, mouth ajar, breathing loosely, cheek gouged against a wooden deck chair slat. He's going to look like someone took a hatchet to his cheekbone when he wakes up. Floyd's son can fall asleep squatting to tie a shoe or spooning in a bowl of cream of wheat. Floyd watches the tilt of Trevor's shoulder blade, the disorderly slide. Making sure he's a second-rate dad exhausts Trevor. Sweet anxiety fizzes up in Floyd. He sucks in peppermint hard. Never had time for Trevor as a kid. Always off laying a foundation, renovating someone's bath. Least he can do is startle up a little fun for Trevor's girls. Least he can do is make like a hopeless dad, an old man, and two girls add up to family. Last night, he set up the cracked croquet set on the lawn. The girls swung their mallets like wild things. Floyd stood around with a drink in his hand, saying things like, "I couldn'ta done much better," each time Trevor screwed up his shot.

Fireworks needle through Floyd's hip. Got shingles in his butt cheek seven years ago and if she doesn't still blast pain. A cigarette, thick with ash, bobs precariously between Trevor's fingers, edging the wooden arm of his deck chair. The kid's had an afternoon nap every day the whole week he's been here. Excursions to dreamland, Floyd calls them. Your father's left us on an excursion to dreamland. Trevor's a good parent, Floyd reckons. Just his ex-wife's better.

Meredith

Jazz, tap, gymnastics, violin, ringette. Rounds the week off with yoga "to meet their inner needs." Christ. The girls are ten and eleven years old! "Downward dog!" Meredith will cry if the girls are slapping each other, and they drop and hold. Meredith got custody because, she informed the judge, Trevor just lets them play. She and the judge held each other's gaze, Meredith in a printed housedress with capped sleeves, the kind of dress — lord knows where she dredged it up. The judge draped in her black robe. Trevor tucked his sneakers under his seat. Well, what can you do with a dad like that?

Meredith's big on Family Meetings where you go around the circle and "express yourself." She calls these meetings after the girls' violin lessons on Saturday afternoons. For a while she took lessons along with them, but violins don't like Meredith much. Squawk and screech at the sight of her. Kouzie doesn't like Meredith much either. Woman's got a fly up her ass, he'll say cheerfully, rolling a cigarette with brown-stained fingers when Floyd bellyaches, though Kouzie's never met the woman. He'll never have to. But she's Floyd's daughter-in-law, the mother of his grandgirls. She divorced Trevor, but Floyd's stuck to her. He walked in on one of her Family Meetings — his first (his last) — passing through one Saturday afternoon. He'd been helping Randy McPherson get rid of dry rot in his garage. Owed him for wiring Floyd's shed. Floyd joined the circle on the living room floor, breathing, staring at Meredith's obscenely long toes.

"How are you feeling?" Meredith inquired. What the fuck? His ass hurt. Couldn't come up with a goddamn thing. Meredith tried again. "How's Astrid feeling?" Lifting a veined hand to display metallic green fingernails. "Haven't felt her yet today," Floyd said. Meredith humped up like a jackass eating thistles, left nostril fluttering. Expelled Floyd from future meetings. Trevor, poor bastard, no such luck.

He's still called back to the house once a month to "express himself." Jesus. Sounds like he's taking a crap.

Floyd was eager to fix things around the house after that Family Meeting. He wanted to putter, make it up to Meredith, for Trevor's sake. But for the first time ever there was nothing in the house to fix. Meredith had taken a course called Women Fix-It, and her textbook hunched ominously on the kitchen counter. *Home Improvement 1,2,3*. Fat son-of-a-bitch. Five hundred-some pages. Still, Floyd waited about in hopes of a leak, an electrical surge, ready to spring to the sink, the dishwasher, at the hint of a gurgle, and so meet with his daughter-in-law's approval. Turns out lurking puts Meredith off.

The tractor scrapes over a croquet hoop sunk into the lawn. Floyd hops off, pulls out his pocketknife and yanks her up while the tractor idles, the girls hurtling back and forth. Floyd waves Carolyn over, hands her the pen and the tally. Let them keep their own score. Improve their math skills. He clatters the hoop against the tractor's wheel hub and off he jolts. All he needs is to send one of the girls home to Meredith with a sprained ankle. Meredith's big on protection. She's big on foreign films. And the woman doesn't believe in cars. Jogs everywhere with that tall-girl stoop some girls learn in high school. Has this giant baby stroller she pushed the girls in when they were tykes. Instead of letting Floyd haul it off to one of his garage sales — Floyd's addicted to garage sales, holds two a month, and damned if he can pass by any lawn piled with someone else's junk — she flings her paraphernalia into the contraption: books, city maps, vacuum cleaner on the blink, birthday gifts, pulls on her cape, and trots, shoving the thing over sidewalks, ruts, killing five birds with one stone. Jogs to the technical college. Jogs to the lumber store. Jogs to parent-teacher interviews. Sprints to her yoga class, sweating and smelly before she gets there. She's like some large flapping crow. She jogged to Video Barn the last time Floyd passed through. Trotted back with an Italian movie with a title no one could pronounce. The movie had subtitles. They were supposed to *read* the movie. Meredith slid the disc in. They all leaned forward, squinting. A woman with rolls around her middle leans over a toilet bowl in a restaurant's grimy bathroom, holding a pair of goddamn tweezers, trying to extract her dangly earring fallen in the toilet. Almost gets it. Drops it. Al-most. Ohhhh. This goes on. While she fishes, the tour bus driver, more fed up than Floyd, leaves without her. She chases the bus in her high-heeled shoes, back end jiggling, can't catch it, so she hitchhikes to Venice. Finds herself. Two and a half hours — finding herself. More painful than shingles. Floyd had to drink. Trevor and Meredith separated eleven days later.

But not before Meredith got serious about Family Yoga. She regularly schedules yoga trips to California, Oregon, New York, cramming her already spilled-over schedule to study under gurus. Trevor's a first-rate dad each time she needs a babysitter. And how does she say thanks? Flies home and uses the lot of them as guinea pigs. Floyd was co-opted into one of her yoga sessions, bending and twisting. When Meredith cried, "Folded leaf pose!" Floyd folded from the waist, breaking wind so enthusiastically, three short rips ascending the scale, that the yoga session fell apart right there. "Toot, Grampa! Gramps tooted!" the little girls shrieked, applauding, while Floyd sat straight-backed, trying for dignified. They reconvened in the kitchen for supper—tofu burgers, salad sprinkled with birdseed, Meredith grim as grime. Floyd is a reasonable man: now when he wants a visit, Trevor brings the girls to him.

The tractor motor's spitting. When did he last fill the thing? Floyd jerks up to the shed and refills her with a jerry can in time to see the girls reappear around the house with homemade green freshie popsicles. There'll be a mess on the kitchen counter.

An orange cat lands on the tractor fender.

Alba

"Hey, Alba!" Best pussy he's ever had, Floyd likes to say. Alba's stuck with him for sixteen years, through two marriages, a bankruptcy, and three polyp removals. Last year, for her fifteenth birthday Floyd flew her to Vegas. What the hell. Cat deserved a holiday—highbrow cat condo on the strip—Purrfect Place—thirty-eight bucks a day. Her own room with TV, Persian rug, and cat bed. Cat massage included. Even had visiting hours. When Floyd dropped her off, the fish-lipped woman behind the counter warned him not to try to visit between two and three p.m.—rest time for the cats. Held up a Do Not Disturb sign to show she meant business. Christ. Floyd doesn't get naps.

Alba takes the short leap and settles in Floyd's lap. "Hi, Alba. Hi, babe." He steers with one hand and rubs her head and down her back, hard, like she likes. Alba snarls, then licks him. Cat's crazy as hell. Like his second wife. Alba's got her rituals. Floyd has to get up early, come down the stairs and rattle Alba's food bowl. Five a.m. even if he filled it the night before. Got to rattle her. Otherwise damned cat won't eat. And she's one ornery female when hungry. Wreaks havoc until he does it. Knocks everything off the bed stand for starters. And that's just her warm up. She gives him five seconds. That doesn't rouse him, she sits on his face. Still not up? Goes at his chest with her claws, purring like a throttle — in case scratching don't work, her engine will. How has his life come to hauling himself out of bed, five in the morning to rattle a goddamn cat bowl? Truth is, he'd once dreamed maybe he'd be lucky enough to drive down whatever stretch of road remains with Roslyn in the passenger seat. His chest splinters — don't think about her — but he's already there. Oh, he had foolish hopes, once upon a time. Sweetest woman he ever met. He'd of barbecued for her, read books to her; well, turns out she didn't want him. His chest so fucking tight, he reaches for his Skoal. He can't deny it — he thought a lot about offering her his acreage — he'd of cleaned it up for her, cleaned himself up for her. But one day, after building his nerve, after he brought her another box of plums — day before, he'd redone her outdoor stair rail and refused to charge her — she took matters into her own hands. Just stood holding the box, saying, gently, "Floyd, Floyd, Floyd," and he knew right there the gig was up. She set the box on the porch floor and led him to her couch — he's never been comfortable in a woman's living room — she held his hands and said she thought the world of him. Hardest thing he ever had to hear. His chest so dry he had to mouth-breathe. He tried to withdraw his hands, get the hell out, but she hung on. Said he was an exemplary human being who she'd always admire — even his arms were shaking. She just squeezed tighter. The problem was, she said — get this — how kind and wonderful he was. She'd been thinking a lot. "You have such a warm heart, Floyd. You collect needy people. And I'm realizing" — she started crying — "I have to stop being one of those." She kissed him, her face was wet, and she said, "Dear Floyd," as if she were writing him a letter, "you're too good for your own good." Talk about kicking a guy when he's down. You can't overcome that. He was fucking screwed.

The lawn tractor rattles over the sewer cover and Floyd jerks the wheel, runs his hand hard over Alba's back, fingers tangling her fur to push down the swell of emptiness busting his ribcage. Doesn't life have a way of veering off just as you reach out to grab her by the tail. So blind he never saw it coming. Well, he'd of never fit in her world. She's an educated lady. And him? He's just a working stiff. He shoves her image away. Pictures Alba, how, when he gets himself a glass of water, Alba stops what she's doing and turns into a stalker. Pins her eyes on his glass. Minute he sets it down, she leaps and stuffs her face into the smaller-than-her-head opening, lapping frantically, eyes pulled squinty like a fish-eye lens. Doesn't even know she's a cat. And he didn't know he was a goddamn fool. Well, what can you do but take what life dispenses? He tries to be grateful for what he's got. Floyd steers the tractor for the grass under the clothesline, breathing in smoke from Alba's fur. She's been sleeping in Astrid's bed. Now *there's* a smoker. All day long. Astrid, in the basement, lighting another cigarette.

Astrid

Astrid's slept in every day she's been here. Floyd glances at his watch. Going on to eleven o'clock. Better check on her. At this rate he'll be mowing lawn until tomorrow. But he could use a drink. Once Astrid's up, she shuffles around for a while before crawling back into bed with her smokes and her romance novels. Floyd steps into his kitchen that's been under construction now for four years. Too busy doing jobs for other people, never gets around to finishing his own. Kind of lost his momentum when Roslyn sent him off howling at the moon. Astrid comes up to Canada once a year now—hates snow, so that leaves July or August. Soon as Trevor and the girls leave, Floyd will drive her home—drove twenty-one and a half hours to pick her up, he'll drive twenty-one and a half to take her back. Well, a man needs something to fill his time. Montana—forests. Utah—burnt-out barren. Nevada—rocky. Cactus-green Arizona. Astrid smoking the whole goddamn way. Can't be left on a plane without lighting up. She's peeing in plastic cups now. Soon as he steps into the house, he sees one abandoned on the begonia planter, and here she comes, shuffling into the kitchen in her slippers, holding another cup full.

"Forget about last night's specimen?" Floyd nods at the begonia planter. Astrid sets hers on the cat climber and bends over in wracking coughs. Jesus. "Keep playin', babe," he tells her. "You gotta keep gambling to come up with a royal flush." She has a doctor's appointment here in Fernie tomorrow, then a specialist's appointment back in Phoenix before the week's end. Each time she visits the doctor, she comes home with more chunks missing—ball of her thumb, a deep scrape off her nose, incision behind her ear.

Floyd reaches, but Astrid waves him away. She's a tough bird. When she and Gerta attended The World of Concrete in Las Vegas, Floyd knew right off he'd caught their eye. He leans against the counter and drinks, listening to his grandgirls' laughter. Astrid disappears into the bathroom coughing. Fairgrounds held six hundred thousand milling people. Five hundred exhibits. Floyd was bent over demonstrating decorative concrete, while a man with a microphone described Floyd's step-by-step procedure as he poured the trowel finish. Floyd was hardly listening, trying not to picture himself. Could feel his tufts of grey hair, damp, sticking out around his cap, his jeans slung low off his skinny ass, gut hanging out the front. He's not one for attention. Nervousness brought on hiccups.

Folks would stop and watch a particular display for few minutes and move on, but Astrid and Gerta stayed. Sunlight shot off Gerta's rhinestone tank top and lasered Floyd's eyes. Whenever he looked over, Gerta waved. Floyd chewed his Dentyne. Hard. He needed a pinch of Skoal. He needed a drink. He kept pouring concrete. Beside Gerta sat Astrid, puffing on a cigarette. People clapped when the demonstration ended and Floyd nodded and yanked down his Honk for Hookers cap and Jesus, if Gerta didn't sashay over, her orange hair springing off her head, scary against her skim-milk freckled skin. Astrid strolled behind, dry and scaly. They took Floyd for drinks at a nearby booth, and after their fifth, Gerta said, "Well Mr. Canada Man! How'd you like to be Astrid's handy man" — eyebrows raised on *handy* —

"in exchange for winters in Arizona?" Astrid smoked while Floyd and Gerta worked out the details. Astrid was having trouble getting things done around the place because of her skin cancer, Gerta said. Astrid smoked. Floyd thought maybe if she put her cigarette down and used two hands she might surprise herself. She had skin cancer head to toe from chasing elementary school kids through sunshine for thirty-five years. Gerta pointed out the scales up and down Astrid's arms and legs. Even her stomach, she said, and she lifted Astrid's T-shirt to reveal two sagging rolls, dry and red. Astrid lit a cigarette off her last one, and said, "So, that's settled." And they all three gambled hard for five days: craps tables, roulette, blackjack, Texas hold'em. They stayed at the Rio, took in the evening shows, shuttled between casinos milling with hundreds of thousands of agitated people, air campy with smoke. Floyd won right off on the machines. Worst thing a gambler can do is win too early. Win ten thousand dollars and you'll spend twenty thousand trying to win ten more. Caesar's Palace. The Paris. Bally's. The Flamingo. They toured Old Vegas and watched the light show. Second night Floyd pulled from his jacket pocket a promotion pamphlet about slot tournaments Kouzie had stuffed in Floyd's pocket before he left. Push buttons fast as you can for three days. Winner takes home a hundred thousand dollars. They gambled so much without eating or sleeping that Floyd was invited to judge the bikini contest at Caesar's Palace. Picked #21 but she didn't win. When they ran out of money, they met a guy in the parking lot who was looking to get himself to Arizona. Had a hundred bucks, he said. Could he hitch a ride in Floyd's truck?

"Let him drive the damn thing. He'll pay the gas that way *and* pay you $100 for the trip!" Gerta suggested. So Alba, Floyd, Gerta and Astrid piled in Astrid's car. Gerta drove. Astrid smoked, and Floyd rode in the back seat all the way to Phoenix, Arizona, wind in his face, not a thought in his head.

Astrid comes out of the bathroom, phlegm rumbling in her throat, and pours a coffee.

"You all right, babe?"

She waves and heads for the basement bedroom: cool air and romance novels. Sheen to her legs. She's rubbed herself down with goose lard like he suggested. Helps to moisturize. The woman's flaking apart. Between the smoke and the goose lard, you can always smell Astrid coming.

The Girls

Lord, Floyd loves those girls. Christ, he'll be glad to see them go. A week with the two of them is like a month-long high-stepping foxtrot marathon. They've dived for turtles in the pond. They've gathered eggs from under Floyd's pecking hens. They've played Boggle and crazy eights. He taught them how to shoot craps. They've cooked venison and dried the leftover meat into jerky for loot bags. They've coloured Easter eggs even though it's August. They've played frozen tag, colour tag, reverse tag, dodging deer, Floyd's bad hip shrieking. He's hung from the barn loft during games of hide and seek. He's the best fucking grandpa on this side of the Rockies. Took the girls to the Jaffray Walmart, what locals call the dump. Three garage sales in a week. Cooked beer chicken on the barbecue, bird listing, beer can up its ass. He gives those girls an education!

Didn't he teach them how to render goose fat?

Astrid

Each time Floyd bumps back and forth over the weedy patch of lawn around the north side of the house, he catches glimpses through the bedroom window—Astrid puffing on a cigarette. "You don't even sleep together anymore?" Roslyn said one day after Astrid had called. "I don't get it — *what* are you with her for?"

"Beats me," Floyd said, his bebopping heart catapulting around his chest. From that day on, he stopped seeing Astrid. Till Roslyn put his hopes to bed.

No point stopping smoking now, Astrid says, and Floyd reckons she's right. The three of them arrived in Arizona — Astrid, Gerta, and him. Floyd could have settled in — weather was great — he was sleeping with her *then*, but Astrid popped out of bed every two hours all night long, stood barefoot in her long-john bottoms, no top, like an Amazon, and smoked. Her house was fifty-nine years old, same age as he was at the time. Every room needed something. Still does. When he takes her back he'll stay a few days, do repairs. Floor coverings, patching, painting, tiles laid. Roof needs fixing, new sinks to replace the leaking ones, fireplace washed.

It was the night smokes and Astrid's parties that got him in the end. Her geezer friends would show up, no warning. Someone'd haul out a record player, scratch the needle across the grooves, and the whole lot of them would stick out their elbows, and shuffle without moving their feet. They drank tumblers of vodka slush and whisky sours and got insulted. They clenched each other in paralyzing holds like rigor mortis. Nobody gave a fuck about Floyd's egg-salad sandwiches, or what the time was. They tried to outdo each other telling stories about some dog who'd got his bollocks amputated or a woman whose trailer blew up and the explosion popped her in a tree. They turned up their hearing aids and the place rang. No point going to bed. Floyd ate dishes of ice cream drenched in vodka.

Pre-Roslyn, all this was.

Roslyn. For a time she had him thinking he might be attractive. They sat one day at her kitchen table having morning coffee, sunlight spilling through her kitchen window, flooding the table between them, and he made some joke about him and Kouzie being old and ugly. She looked at him with those grey eyes and said, "You're not ugly, Floyd."

Floyd reaches for his Skoal.

Fifth week of that time in Arizona, Astrid went missing for seventy-two hours. She drove Floyd's truck—her car was in the shop—to the hospital to visit her friend Joyce, who was clipped on her motorized scooter and became a vegetable. Astrid made it to the hospital, because she phoned Floyd to ask how to spell Lithuanians. She was trying to get Joyce interested in an idea for a board game. Astrid's story, when she reappeared, involved a stolen truck (Floyd's), a box of squashed tomatoes, and a side trip to Tucson, some drinking, which left nineteen hours unaccounted for. Astrid's glasses were broken but other than that she seemed all right. She said, What's the capital of Latvia?, went straight to the basement and started typing. Floyd stood at the top of the stairs but couldn't think of a single thing to holler down.

Astrid sat in the basement seven hours a day, typing letters to the editor of the *Phoenix Republic* with one finger, irritated suggestions of how the mayor might improve Phoenix's garbage pick-up or its scenic rest stops. She began each letter with an explanation about her schoolteacher education and years of experience, and why most people might value her opinions, then moved on to how to improve Phoenix's parks (install feline water slides), its sewage treatment plant (give Canadians tours), its anti-terrorist drills (something involving paintball). Astrid wanted to run her suggestions past Floyd, who was then supposed to argue the other side. But Floyd was terrible at arguing. It's why two wives left him. He could never think up a reason they should stay.

Once the police located his truck, Floyd got in it, drove to the Circle K to get the *Phoenix Republic,* left Astrid shouting up the landing about whether she wanted the tiles in her kitchen laid, diamond or square. He picked up a carton of 2%, stopped to play the one-arm bandit, won twenty bucks, filled up with gas and drove onto Greenway Parkway, then 7th Avenue. He hit the 101 Freeway just after morning rush hour and took it through Wikeupi (Floyd liked to call it Wakie Uppie). Only six hours to Vegas. What the hell. He cruised right through and didn't stop till he'd crossed the border and was back on his own cluttered patch of heaven in the BC Rockies. Home felt like shade after days of sunburn.

They've kept visiting each other, except for the year he worked for Roslyn. It's only in the last three months that Astrid has deteriorated so. Floyd goes back outside, cuts around the garden, jolts the tractor into the shed, and turns her off. He hears an engine belching up the lane. Kouzie's motorcycle. Floyd leans over, picks a carrot from his wire-fenced vegetable patch and hands it to Amelia skipping past. "Ewwww! We don't eat food with *dirt* on it!" she says. Floyd takes a bite, walks past snoring Trevor, around the house onto his front deck, and looks through the open door. A porcupine is in the kitchen, eating from the cat's dish, Alba humped and hissing on the counter top. "Get," Floyd says without much enthusiasm. He never shuts doors in summer. Summer's too short. Screen door fell apart two springs ago and he can't get around to installing the new one. Floyd loves the puzzle of renovating someone else's house. The meticulous planning, sometimes a rebuild from the foundation up. Picture on a piece of paper spiralling to life. But his own shit — Floyd looks around at his patchy drywall, unpainted ceiling, exposed beams, missing cupboard doors. Can't get wound up and at 'er.

Alba throws Floyd a scornful glance and stalks off across the stove. The porcupine lumbers regretfully toward the sliding glass doors and onto the deck, mouth pinched in irritation. Puts Floyd in mind of Meredith. It lowers itself over the side as Kouzie's motorcycle bumps to a halt on Floyd's asphalt driveway.

Kouzie

Kouzie hauls himself off his bike as best a man with swollen legs can haul. He's dangling two twenty-dollar bills.

"Twenty bucks for the winner!" he calls.

Kouzie surprised Floyd by giving notice a few months back on the house of Floyd's Kouz was renting in Fernie. Bought himself a little piece of land up at Ty Lake, he said. Could Floyd build him a three-car garage? Floyd knows Ty Lake like he knows the inside of a lumber store. He built most of the million-dollar properties hugging the lakeshore. Turns out did one for Roslyn's sister before he ever met Roslyn. Floyd scrapes off a bit of Skoal. Kouzie's property? A swampy bit of cove, edged by glass-eyed mansions.

"Where you going to put the house?" Floyd asked a few weeks later out at the property as Kouzie stamped out the perimeter of the garage.

"What house?" Kouzie sang, plopping down on his motorcycle like it was an easy chair. He gestured at a lop-sided little bunkhouse with a tin roof hiding in the trees. "I've moved in a cot and a chair. It's comfy as hell. My galvanized ghetto!" Kouzie scratched happily. "No decent woman would want to move in! Not even Mother."

"Your washroom?"

Kouzie waved in the general direction of the campground.

"Washing machine?"

"Why, the lake!" Kouzie said. "I fling 'em in the lake. If they come back, they're clean. I'm not having me one of them newfangled European washers that are all the rage — Swedish. Hold two T-shirts and a sock. My method's better.

Buy a few hundred items at the Sally Ann. Throw the dirty ones in garbage bags I keep out back. Fling a pile in the lake every three, four months. Don't come back, I head to Sally Ann, buy me a whole new wardrobe."

"Twenty bucks for the winner!" Kouzie hollers. The girls come running.

The Girls

Kouzie throws his arms wide and gathers in them in. "Jesus! You girls smell like shit!"

"Winner of what?" Carolyn puffs, jumping for the money.

"We're playing Poop-Pick-Up!" Amelia announces.

"Whose poop? Your grandpa's?"

"No!" The girls roll on the newly-mowed lawn, laughing and staining their clothes. "The deer!"

"What're the rules?" Kouzie limps toward the picnic table.

"We pick up deer poop!"

"With our toes! It's gotta be with our toes or Gramps won't pay up."

"Twenty-five cents a drop!" Carolyn points at the two old pails Floyd rolled out from the shed.

"And no Ewwww-ing! Or we don't get our money!" Amelia hollers.

"Well, that game stinks!" Kouzie falls onto the picnic bench. "Where does your Gramps fit in?"

Trevor appears blearily around the side of the house, an angry red gouge pressed into the skin beneath his eye. Floyd dekes into the kitchen to get the kid a beer.

"Gramps is the Game Master!"

"I see," Kouzie says. "Well, I have a better idea. Twenty bucks for the winner o-o-of—" He does a drum roll. "Who Can Most Annoy YOUR DAD!"

Trevor lasts all of ten minutes before making a dash to his truck and speeding off down the lane. To the Red Bull, Floyd imagines.

"Guess it'll be Who Can Most Annoy Your Grampa!"

"Keep your money, Kouzie. You've already won." Floyd drops into the adjacent lawn chair and rubs grass blades off his neck and arms. Kouzie sits back with a happy sigh and rolls himself a cigarette.

Forty minutes later, Kouzie declares a tie and passes out the bills. Floyd sinks onto the deck, toenails twinkling sparkly fluorescent blue, red felt-marker tattoos up and down his arms, elastics and barrettes launching short grey pigtails off his head. The girls pile on top of him. He and Kouzie are finishing their fourth beer when Trevor weaves unsteadily up the drive, parks against a tree, and tells the girls he's had a call from their mother. It's time to pack up and take them back to Kamloops.

Floyd shakes a pinch of Skoal out of his tin.

"Can we have a flower from your garden, Gramps?"

"No room for extras," Trevor says.

Floyd stuffs the wad into his cheek.

"We want something to remember Gramps by!" Amelia wheedles.

"Christ. Is he dead?" Kouzie blows a smoke ring. Floyd picks two tiger lilies, shakes the dirt off their wire stems and fetches the venison jerky, left butt cheek shooting forked lightning. He has a sudden urge to shove a bouquet of gladioli into Trevor's hands, but Trevor is hauling suitcases to the truck and that'd just be lame.

"You shouldn't chew tobacco, Grampa," Carolyn says primly, accepting her flower through the open truck window, looking unnervingly like Meredith.

"He doesn't *chew* tobacco," Amelia says bossily, leaning around her. "He slurps it. You slurp —"

The truck is rolling down the drive. Floyd's sight goes blurry. The two men wave until the truck disappears into the trees.

Kouzie

"A beer with a friend. No better way to spend a Monday afternoon!" Kouzie limps across the deck and eases his bulky self down into the lawn chair facing the shed.

"Tuesday," Floyd says. "It's Tuesday, Kouz." Kouzie's cheeks are off-kilter-pink, like light reflected in oil. Floyd heads into the kitchen.

"That's the great thing about working for yourself, Floyd," Kouzie calls after him. "What day it is don't matter."

Floyd steps back out sideways through the sliding glass doors with two bottles, the toaster, and half a loaf of raisin bread. "Fix you a bite?"

"Never eat on an empty stomach, Floydo." Kouzie checks his watch. "I do believe I've slept through Monday! *Lovely* way to start the week. Look at your orchard." Four deer and a fawn are staggering about on their hind legs, picking plums with their teeth.

"They'll be shitting them out the other end in no time," Floyd says, plugging the toaster into the deck wall.

Kouzie swings one leg up on the picnic bench and Floyd sucks in hard. The skin between Kouzie's shoe and pant leg is mottled purple-black. Two crusty open sores ooze above the ankle.

Floyd's hand goes for his back pocket. He drops two slices of raisin bread in the toaster, and takes a pinch. The deer wander over and wait in a polite semi-circle. After some hoof-shuffling, one breaks from the herd and steps forward to nibble the last of Amelia's egg and bacon that's been drying to the plate since breakfast. "Seen a doctor?" Floyd nods in the direction of Kouzie's foot, keeps himself busy, buttering toast.

"Floydo, doctors don't know shit."

Kouzie shakes his head at Floyd's offering so Floyd breaks the pieces onto the picnic table and the rest of the deer clop onto the deck and help themselves.

"Woman in the blue house on the curb?" Kouzie says. "Three up from me? Number one-sixty-nine?? Sells compressors out of her house? You can't really offend her much. Told her the joke about the priest and the goat—anyways, she was a nurse's aide way back. Says it's nothing they can't fix. 'That's just a little ol' ulcer,' she says." Kouzie taps his pant leg with a split thumbnail. After some silence. "Nothing that woman can't fix but a broken heart." And after a while, "And maybe the crack o' dawn." They sit silent for a while. "You missed the party at the autobody last night, Floydo. You missed the sing-song. What're those trails of slime down your cupboard doors?" Kouzie's peering through the open sliding door.

"Snails. Girls picked 'em at the pond."

"Snotty buggers, aren't they?"

Floyd says. "I'll clean 'em later."

"Uh-huh," Kouzie says.

"Hurt much?" Floyd nods again at Kouzie's blackened foot.

"Have to head back soon, do my rounds," Kouzie says. "Those rich Calgarians got me walking their properties, checking for jimmied locks. They pay you to build their mansions, Floydo, and me they pay the whole goddamn year to be their guard dog. Hurt? Naw. Itches. Forget about it. I've started up a little bottle depot business. Selling beer to the Calgarians. Buy 'er for a song over the Alberta border, cash in on the empties. Empties alone should bring me twenty thousand dollars, I figure. Plan to recycle eighty-two thousand cans of beer this year." Kouzie's toe scratches up his pant leg, fast, like a dog.

"Been to the Walmart, I see," Floyd says, gesturing to the contraption Kouzie has tied into his sidecar.

"Prairie people, they're crazy," Kouzie says. "Drop the damndest things off before they head back across the border. Half of it's brand new: wine presses, crock pots, blood-pressure monitors, Epson Stylus 3200 printers, cookie sheets, two-by-fours. Never know when a scrap of corrugated tin or an old meat grinder might come in handy. You get the girls anything?" Kouzie says. "Sweet things, aren't they?"

"I let 'em pick. Came home with a wheelchair," Floyd says, "a 250-gallon fuel tank, a nail bin, and a washing machine barrel. Trevor? Goddamn city kid. 'Dad, what would I want this junk for?' he says. 'See these cubby holes?' I told him." Floyd holds up a nail bin lying against the deck. "Drill some holes. Give 'er a front and you've got yourself a birdcage. That old washing machine? Make a fine fire pit. No interest."

"Nice kid, no imagination," Kouzie says. "Course he'll have to chuck the lot," Kouzie's wave takes in Floyd's acreage, "when you go belly up. Cash in your chips."

"Not plannin' to for a while, Kouzie," Floyd says. "You?"

Kouzie grimaces, and walks to his bike, pats the roped-on contraption. "Got me this brand new air conditioner this morning. Bury it with me, Floydo, case I go to hell. It was sitting on top of a deep freeze, givin' me the eye. Shit, Floyd, here we are, dabbling in junk from the goddamn dump, and look at Ditmer up the road, that Dutchman. Sold his farm to the Hutterites for three-point-five million. His latest project? Rocks. Why didn't we thinka rocks? Just sitting there. A mountainside of rocks. He sells 'em on the prairie. Those bastards from Saskatchewan are crazy about rocks. Rock as big as your lounge chair there sells for fifteen hundred bucks!"

"You don't need money," Floyd says.

"Don't need women neither. But I like 'em," Kouzie scratches. His fingernails come away red. "But some dreams you gotta give up on. I tried the marrying stuff, Floydo. Worked out for a while. But they just play me out. Third wife was twenty years younger'n me. That one nearly took me down. By the time she was done with me, I was just nuts and rib cage hangin' out." Kouzie coughs. "Might sell my property, Floydo. Get myself a school bus. Live in the bush. I don't much use the lake, 'cept for washing. Daughter's broke again. Beggin' for cash. I been thinking. I could buy me two hundred T-shirts at the Sally Ann and I'd only have to wash every six months. Besides, I spend my mornings sleeping, afternoons I walk the properties, evenings at the autobody with the boys. I don't need scenery." Kouzie coughs, broken and deep. "Party tonight, Floyd." Kouzie wanders around Floyd's deck. "Might be the last time I see you for a while. Thinkin' I might get on my motor-sickle tomorrow. Take the side roads, see some towns I never seen."

Kouzie plunks down suddenly. His breaths sound wet. Christ. Floyd reaches for his Skoal. "I'll be there, Kouz. I'll come."

"We'll be singin', me 'n' Mel. The boys'll start gathering around eight o'clock."

Last night Floyd woke at three a.m., stepped onto the deck for a piss under the stars, and heard Kouzie and Mel, voices floating across the field. He pulled up a lawn chair, just him and a bottle of his homemade plum wine, listening to the coyotes harmonize to "She's Not You."

"Look at your flower garden, Floydo. Now that garden's gonna last." Kouzie grunts to his feet. Sweat breaks on his forehead. He sits back down. Breathes a moment. "Hell. Too early to do any work today. Why, it's not even supper time. What say we settle in, open a bottle of your plum wine, start the party early? Come on, Floydo. It'll be our good luck charm. And a-one and a-two and —"

"You'll scare the deer," Floyd says. Alba bounds onto the deck, rubs hard against Kouzie's legs.

"Get!" Floyd takes the spray hose to a startled Alba, shooting the cat away, then turns his back, spraying, spraying his flower garden.

"Let's have us that drink there, Floydo."

Floyd reaches; his tin comes up empty. Trevor. Those little girls, heading down the highway. Astrid in the basement, lighting another cigarette. Roslyn, with some guy who deserves her. Now Kouzie. Christ.

"Floydo," Kouzie says, so quiet Floyd can hardly hear. "I think I've rolled a 7."

Floyd's hand shakes as he pours. Goddamn you, Kouzie, he thinks. You play. That's what a gambler does. He plays. You fucking keep on playing.

Acknowledgements

My deepest gratitude to Barb Scott, my esteemed editor for the press, for your expert editing and your impressive ability to kick butt while cheering me on. Your respect for language and vision made our many (many!) conversations pure pleasure.

Thank you also:

JoAnn McCaig, Kelsey Attard, and the Freehand gang for so enthusiastically embracing *Are You Ready to Be Lucky?*

Zsuzsi Gartner, for your eagle eye edits and your enthusiastic support of my writing.

Lisa Moore, Susan Musgrave, Karen Solie, and Glen Huser, for sharing your love of writing.

Suzette Mayr and Nicole Markotić, yet again, for your editorial expertise.

Susan MacCulloch, for listening.

Claudia Espinosa, Rena Paul, Rosslyn Clark, and Betty Thompson for talking to me in Spanish, Polish and Scots.

Lloyd Filimek, for teaching me about building, and for your stories.

Loopy Madoff, for your stories.

Tom Dilworth, for generously letting me steal an idea here and there. Alistair MacLeod, for your jokes. And both for our ongoing writerly discussions.

Marilyn and Dan Roth, for graciously offering me your cliff-top Pender paradise to write part of this book.

My children, Madeleine Nixon Stewart and Ryan Stewart, Jordan Nixon and Kelsey Hough, for your love, your senses of humour, your enthusiasm for living, your stories. And your amazing writing gift that helped me complete this book.

Thank you as well to the University of Windsor, and the many professors, students, and secretaries in the English Department who created a warm, supportive, happy environment that made working on this book a pleasure. I miss you still.

Thank you to the University of British Columbia.

Thank you to the Canada Council for the Arts and to the Alberta Foundation for the Arts for your financial support, and the Leighton Colony at The Banff Centre for the Arts for the haven you offer."

"In Which Jesus Hitchhikes the N332 and the Girl Tries Not to Vanish" was published in an earlier version in *Boulderpavement*.

"Left" was published in an earlier version in *The Nashwaak Review*.

"The Sewers of Paris" was published in an earlier version in *Alberta Views*, under the title "Treading."

Rosemary Nixon is a short story writer, novelist, and free-lance writer. Her collection *Mostly Country* was shortlisted for the Howard O'Hagan Award. Her collection *The Cock's Egg* won the Howard O'Hagan Award. Her novel *Kalila* was shortlisted for the Georges Bugnet Award. She has published in literary magazines across Canada and discovered the beginnings of *Are You Ready to Be Lucky?* on a fellowship at Hawthornden Castle, Scotland. Her home is in Calgary.